"But I'm not married."

Tory continued, "And the grant is for married women only."

"That's where I come in," J.D. spoke up. "I'm going to marry you."

"This is crazy," Tory whispered. "Me, marry you?"

"What's wrong, Tory?" J.D. asked in a slow, careful tone. "You said you were willing to do *anything* to get what you want."

"Anything *sane*," she answered. "And legal. Pretending to be married to you would amount to committing fraud."

"But we won't be pretending," he countered easily.

Digging her nails into her palms, Tory wanted to slap that smirk off his face. She had the sinking suspicion she was being manipulated by a master. She just couldn't figure out what J.D. really wanted from her...

Dear Reader,

Welcome to **Shadows & Spice**! More than food and drink are served at The Rose Tattoo, a friendly bar/restaurant in historic Charleston, South Carolina. There's a double dose of danger and desire on the menu, as well.

Kelsey Roberts brings her deft touch for mystery and romance to this suspenseful trilogy. Last month we brought you *Unspoken Confessions*, and this month it's *Unlawfully Wedded*. Look for *Undying Laughter* next month and become a regular at The Rose Tattoo!

Enjoy!

The Editors

Unlawfully Wedded

KELSEY ROBERTS

♥ SILHOUETTE

Intrigue

*First published in Great Britain 1996
by Silhouette Books, Eton House, 18-24 Paradise Road,
Richmond, Surrey TW9 1SR*

© Rhonda Harding Pollero 1995

Silhouette, Silhouette Intrigue and Colophon are
Trade Marks of Harlequin Enterprises II B.V.

ISBN 0 373 22330 7

46-9605

Made and printed in Great Britain

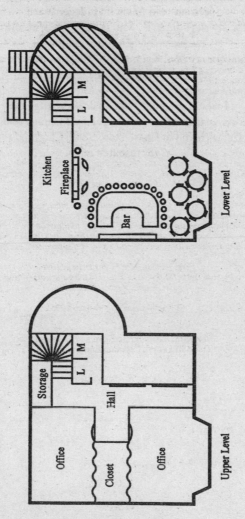

THE ROSE TATTOO

Storage

L | M

Hall

Office

Closet

Office

Upper Level

Kitchen

Fireplace

L | M

Bar

Lower Level

For my stepdaughter, Bonnie, who has achieved
personal and financial independence;
for my stepson, Eric, who is quite adept at selling
his plasma when times get tough;
and for my son, Kyle, who will continue to be on
the dole for the foreseeable future.

I would gratefully like to acknowledge the
assistance of Pat Harding, Kay Manning and
Carol Keane of Charleston, South Carolina: my
crack research team.

Chapter One

J. D. Porter. She knew the initials stood for "Jackass Deluxe," and he was sitting at a table in her station!

A frown curved the corners of her mouth as she donned an air of false confidence. Brushing a few strands of hair away from her eyes, Tory Conway pushed through the hinged kitchen doors of the Rose Tattoo, a tray clamped tightly to her chest.

With practiced aloofness, she held her breath as she marched past where he sat hunched over a mound of paperwork. The pleasant smell of his decidedly masculine cologne chased her behind the bar, threatening her resolve.

After placing the tray on the polished wooden surface of the horseshoe-shaped bar, Tory bent down and began collecting the salt and pepper shakers.

Her motion was halted in midstream when she felt long, tapered fingers close around her wrist. She rose slowly, trying not to devote too much thought to the devastating feel of his touch.

Their eyes collided—hers wide from the shock, his a deep, penetrating gray, the same shade as a South Carolina summer sky before a violent storm. She swallowed against the irrational belief that those eyes could see through her clothing. His lopsided, sexy display of even white teeth hovered somewhere very near a leer.

"Good morning, Miss Conway."

Not from where I'm standing, she thought. She didn't speak immediately, mostly because she had a sinking feeling that her words might come out in a squeaky, helium-high voice.

"No greeting?" he taunted, one dark eyebrow arched questioningly. "You wound me."

"No," she returned with a sweet smile. "But I'd be happy to, as soon as I've finished my setup."

"Ouch," he returned easily, placing his free hand over his heart.

Or, she thought, where his heart would be if he actually had one.

Annoyance crept up her spine when he refused her subtle request to be released when she gave his hand a small tug. "I have work to do," she insisted through tight lips.

"So do I," he said in a frustratingly calm voice that was just too smooth, too velvety to have emanated from such a massive man.

"Then why don't you do it?"

The smile widened, accentuating the chiseled perfection of his angled features. "Would you like to do it? I'm game if you are."

Tory groaned and sucked in a breath in exasperation. The man was infuriating. "Not in your lifetime, Sparky."

The sound of his laugh was deep, rich. It caressed her ears and made her skin tingle. "Haven't you heard of sexual harassment?" she managed to say between her clenched teeth.

"Doesn't apply," he returned easily. "You don't work for me."

"Thank God and anyone else responsible," she grumbled. His hold on her wrist was getting on her nerves. She didn't like being touched, especially by the visiting Neanderthal.

"You aren't very friendly for a waitress, Miss Conway."

"Depends on the customer," she retorted.

"No wonder you can't live off what you earn in tips."

She bristled and might have stiffened her spine had it not been for the unfortunate fact that she had not yet fastened the top button of her uniform. The last thing she wanted, or needed, was to give *Mr. Deluxe* an eyeful of cleavage. Especially since he'd no doubt take it as a come-on.

"I live just fine," she promised him. "And thanks for asking. Your concern is touching."

"I'm not concerned, but I'd be happy to touch." The last half of his statement was delivered in a low, sensual pitch that made her want to scream.

"Come on, J.D.," she pleaded after a brief pause. "Can the double entendre and let me get ready for the lunch crowd."

His eyes dropped to where his dark fingers encircled her small wrist. She followed his lead. His tanned, weathered complexion was a stark contrast to her pale skin. The grip loosened until all she was aware of was the feather-light stroke of his fingertip as it traced the pattern of small bones in her hand.

Tory snatched her hand away, feeling her face flush as the sound of his chuckle reached her ears. The man was maddening, she thought, fuming as she slammed various containers on the top of the bar. He was egotistical. He had enough arrogance for ten men, and he was the most attractive man she'd seen in all her twenty-five years.

My hormones are probably suffering from some sort of deprivation reaction, she reasoned as she arranged the half-empty jars and bottles on her tray.

Trying to ignore J.D.'s presence as she worked was like trying to ignore a rocket launch. Her peripheral vision was filled with images of his broad shoulders and that unruly mass of jet black hair he kept raking his fingers through as he quietly studied the piles of documents spread before him on the table. The worn fabric of his denim shirt clung to the definition of well-muscled arms. One booted toe kept time to the Elvis tune playing on the jukebox.

She didn't like him—hadn't from that very first day. J.D. was one of those stuck-up, abrupt sorts. His expression was always cool, aloof, giving her the impression that he somehow felt he was superior to the whole world. She guessed his attitude might have something to do with the truckloads of money he earned as one of Florida's premier architects. Or, she thought glibly, it could just be the result of his being one of the most gorgeous men on the face of the earth.

"Tory!"

She turned in the direction of the familiar female voice, her eyes homing in on her boss's harsh features. Rose Porter leaned against the kitchen door, her heavily jeweled hand patting the stiff mass of blond hair lacquered against her head.

"Yes?"

"There's a guy here for you."

Tory pointedly ignored J.D.'s apparent interest in Rose's announcement. The woman's stiletto heels clicked against the wood-planked floor as she held the door open wide.

Tory smiled as she caught sight of Dr. Mitchell Greyson, dean of student services at Oglethorpe College. Dr. Greyson shuffled in, his small body listing to the side where his hand toted a sizable briefcase. The scent of witch hazel reached her a fraction of a second before the rumpled, balding man. His appearance sent signals of disaster surging through her. Greyson only left his office to deliver bad news. She braced herself against the table. . . .

"Miss Conway," he greeted in his proper southern accent. "I'm sorry to trouble you at your place of employment."

Tory's grin grew wider. She was a waitress, not the CEO of some fancy corporation. Greyson acted as if he'd interrupted important merger negotiations.

"No problem," she told him brightly, tucking a dish towel into the waistband of her apron. Gesturing to one of the chairs, Tory offered him a seat as she glared at J.D. He was leaning back in his chair, watching her as if she were the main feature at the theater.

J.D.'s expression didn't falter when their eyes briefly met. That bothered her.

"I'm afraid I have some rather distressing news," Dr. Greyson began as he sat down and placed his briefcase on the table, then slowly extracted a crisp, white sheet of letterhead, which he handed to her.

Taking the letter, Tory's eyes scanned the neatly typed print. She read it again, sure she had somehow misconstrued its meaning.

"This isn't possible," she managed to say in a strangled voice.

Rose came over then, standing behind her with one hand comfortingly resting on Tory's shoulder.

"What does it mean?" Rose asked.

"I'm dead," Tory answered as the full impact of the news settled over her like a heavy blanket.

"Not necessarily," Dr. Greyson cut in. "I've brought along a directory of college funding," he said, pulling a tattered paperback from his briefcase.

Tory groaned. "I've been all through that. I couldn't find a single one I qualified for."

"Perhaps there are some new listings?" Greyson suggested.

"Maybe," she responded dismally.

"You know," Greyson said as he patted the back of her hand with his pudgy fingers. "You can take a year or so off. Perhaps by then the 'forces that be' will reinstate the program."

"Maybe," Tory repeated.

"I'll keep my ears open," Greyson promised as he scooted his chair back and rose to his modest height. "Perhaps the board of trustees . . ."

Of course, she knew the board could do nothing on her behalf.

"I'm finished," Tory whispered, expelling an anguished sigh.

"Can we help?" Rose asked, taking the seat Greyson had vacated. "Shelby and I—"

"Are hardly in a position to cough up seventeen thousand dollars," Tory finished. "Shelby has Chad and she's expecting another baby any minute. And I know you have all your cash committed to the rehab of the outbuildings. Until you finish the work on the dependencies, you aren't in any condition to loan me money."

Rose's painted red lips thinned and she adjusted the black leather belt cinching her waist. She reached forward and grabbed the directory that Dr. Greyson had left behind.

"Forget it." Tory shrugged. "I've already maxed out my eligibility for student loans, along with every grant and scholarship known to mankind."

"But you haven't even tried to find alternative funding," Rose argued with a snort.

"Rose," Tory began slowly. "All you'll find in that directory is a bunch of weird stuff. Scholarships for blue-eyed women with Spanish surnames born in the month of May. Grants for anyone born under the same star as some philanthropist's Maltese."

She followed the sound of the deep, throaty chuckle. Having J. D. Porter laugh when her whole world was shattering didn't sit well.

"Amused?" she asked tartly. "I'm so glad you find my crisis funny." She stood and braced her hands on her hips. "I need some air," she told Rose. "If I don't get away from him, I might just take out my frustrations on your useless son."

She stormed out of the room, the vision of J.D.'s dancing gray eyes vividly etched in her brain. He had laughed at her! She fumed as she stepped into the early-June humidity. What kind of unfeeling jerk would laugh at a time like this? "Jackass Deluxe," she grumbled as she stalked through the overgrown gardens behind the property.

The tall, damp grass licked at her ankles above her socks, leaving a sheen of moisture on her white aerobic shoes. The air was thick with the scent of the wild vines growing along the brick exterior of the dependency.

The scent inspired memories from the past. Memories of when her family had owned this place. She had been a ten-year-old princess and this had been her kingdom. Her hand reached out to touch the coolness of the weather-beaten stone wall. A small lizard skittered along the surface, then disappeared behind the growth of vegetation threatening to overtake the dilapidated building.

She was thrilled that Rose and Shelby had decided to restore the outbuilding of the Charleston single house. The dependency, which had once served as both kitchen and servants quarters, had been neglected for more than a hundred years. Her only misgiving was the man hired to do the work.

J. D. Porter was an architect known for his dramatic, modern structures. She frowned, imagining what Mr. Steel-and-Glass Towers might do to this historically significant structure. Cringing, she allowed her fingers to admire the stone. J.D. didn't appreciate or even understand historical preservation. He didn't appreciate Rose, either. He was charging his own mother an hourly rate for the renovation. "That man is a piece of work."

"Thanks."

Tory spun around and her hand flew to her mouth. Wide-eyed, she looked into the relaxed face and instantly felt her cheeks burn. "I didn't...hear you," she stammered.

J.D. shifted so that his large body cast a long shadow over Tory. Deep lines appeared on either side of his eyes as he squinted against the sunlight.

"I take it you're being squeezed out of the world of academe."

Tory felt her shoulders slump forward. "It seems that way."

"What will you do?"

She shrugged and dropped her gaze to the front of his shirt. It was a stupid move, she realized too late. Her eyes lingered at the deep V where he'd neglected to button his shirt. A thick mat of dark hair curled over solid, tanned skin. She swallowed and forced her eyes to the ground.

"I may have to wait a year or so until I can get another grant."

He shifted his weight again as his thumbs looped into the waistband of his jeans. "What about your family? Can't they help with your tuition?"

"Interesting concept, coming from you," she said as she met his eyes. "I don't really have any family." Needing to change the subject, Tory asked, "How can you charge your own mother top dollar?"

His expression grew dark, and something vaguely dangerous flashed in his eyes. "I'm a businessman, Tory. Not a philanthropist."

Heartless creep! her mind screamed. "She's your mother."

"Biologically," he qualified.

"It still counts," Tory told him with a saccharine smile.

Lifting sunglasses from the breast pocket of his shirt, J.D. placed them on the bridge of his slightly crooked nose. Tory was left to view her own reflection in their mirrored lenses.

"Want to give me a hand?"

"What?" she fairly squealed.

Her voice caused an immediate smile to cut the sharp angles of his face. "Assist me?"

"Doing what *exactly?*"

"I'm open for suggestions," he countered with a wolfish grin.

"And I'm outta here," she answered as she took her first step.

"Hey," he said as his large hand closed around her arm. "I was just teasing you. No need to get huffy."

"I don't care for your brand of teasing, J.D. Everything that comes out of your mouth has some sort of sexual meaning behind it."

"I'll behave," he promised, one hand raised in an oath.

"I'll bet," she told him wearily.

"Honest. I just want you to hold the tape while I measure." He produced a shiny metal tape measure in support of his statement. "I need to get the dimensions of the outhouse so I can finish that ream of paperwork the historical society requires."

"It isn't an outhouse. It's called a dependency. And the forms are necessary," she told him with great hauteur in her voice. "We have to maintain the historical fabric of the city."

His mouth thinned in a definite sneer. "Just because something is old, that doesn't make it worth saving."

"I'd save you, Mr. Porter."

"Think I'm old, huh?"

"Not old," she said with an exaggerated bat of her long lashes. "Historically significant."

The skin of her upper arm tingled where his fingers gently held her. It was annoying that she felt herself respond to him, but she silently vowed not to show any reaction. She suspected J.D. would enjoy knowing his touch affected her—and she wasn't about to give him that much power.

"Will you?"

"What?" she answered, wondering if he had psychic powers in his arsenal.

"Help me measure."

"It's almost noon," she hedged. "The lunch crowd cometh."

"So does Susan."

"Susan isn't working this shift."

"She is now," he stated. "Rose thought you might like to take the afternoon off in light of your sudden financial upheaval."

"How is losing a day's tips supposed to make me feel better?"

Nodding his dark head, J.D. used his free hand to stroke the faint growth on his deeply clefted chin. "Good point. Tell you what," he said with a sigh, as if he were about to announce a change in world leaders. "I'll pay you the going rate for helping me measure."

"How generous," she gasped. "Sure you can spare seven-fifty an hour?"

He leaned down, so close that Tory could feel the warmth of his breath against her ear. "For you? Anything."

Her resolve not to react to this man disintegrated when the scent of his cologne lingered in the mere inches separating them. Shrugging away from him, Tory could still feel the imprint of his callused fingers against her skin. A smart person would cut and run. But then, a woman with less than a hundred dollars in the bank didn't always act intelligently.

"Has your mother already called Susan?"

"Yes, Rose called."

She stifled the urge to ask him why he wouldn't call Rose "mom" or "mother." "Then give me the tape."

Reaching behind him, J.D. again produced the tape measure as well as a folded sketch of the dependency's exterior. "Here," he said, handing her the drawing and a mechanical pencil. "We'll start on the south wall. We'll measure it, then you mark the drawing."

"Fine," Tory said. She kept the bent end of the tape between her fingers as he took long strides through the dense foliage. He had a great derriere, she mused. Tight and rounded above those long, muscular legs. Absently, she fanned herself with the sketch, trying to convince herself that the heat she felt in the pit of her stomach was probably nothing more than the effect of having drunk too much coffee.

The strip of metal tape acted like an umbilical cord, connecting her to the large man. Dutifully, she followed his instructions as they spent the better part of an hour documenting the contours of the old building. She attributed her dry throat to the stifling early-summer heat. It couldn't possibly have anything to do with the fact that her eyes had been riveted to his body the entire hour. She wasn't the type to be interested in things like the washboard-like muscles of his flat stomach, or the gentle slope of his back where his broad shoulders tapered at his waist. No—such things were irrelevant to a woman like Tory.

"You look hot."

"I beg your pardon?" she yelped.

His smile was slow and deliberate. "I was referring to the temperature." He swabbed his forehead with the back of his hand. "It must be near ninety."

"Must be," she agreed as she swallowed her guilt.

"Need a break before we tackle the interior?"

"Not me," she told him. She wanted to get this over with—quickly. "The inside is a disaster."

"I know. I took a cursory look when I was putting together the budget for the project."

"I'm sure your estimate was high," she said without looking at him.

"I'm sure it was reasonable."

Ignoring the slight edge to his voice, Tory moved to the near-rotten door and grasped the knob. The door wouldn't budge.

"Let me," J.D. said, coming up behind her so that his thighs brushed her back.

Tory stepped out of his way almost instantly, feeling branded by the outline of his body.

J.D. wrestled with the humidity-swollen door for a short time before finally pulling it free of the frame. Reaching into his back pocket, he produced a small flashlight and directed the beam in front of them.

The air inside the building was stale and musty. "Let's start on the left," J.D. suggested.

The interior was a long, rectangular-shaped space with bowed stone walls and a few rotted timbers piled at the far end. Bars of yellow light filtered in from the boarded windows, imprisoning J.D. as he placed the measure against what was left of the old flooring.

"Sixty-three feet, seven inches," he called.

Tory was about to mark the diagram when she noted the inconsistency. "The tape must be twisted."

She heard his boots scrape as he checked the length of the tape. "Nope."

"Then that back wall is three feet deep," she told him.

J.D. took the sketch from her, his eyebrows drawn together as he looked from the drawing to the room, then back to the paper.

"This doesn't make sense."

"You must have measured incorrectly."

He offered her a baleful stare before walking off to the back of the room. "Hold this," he called, handing her the flashlight as she came up behind him.

Using his pocketknife as well as his fingers, J.D. loosened the stones by scraping away the limestone mortar.

"What are you doing?" Tory asked.

"I'm trying to find the other three feet."

An oddly unpleasant odor accompanied the shower of small rocks as he created a small opening in the wall.

"Give me the light."

J.D. stuck his arm through the opening, then she heard him suck in his breath.

"What?"

His arm came out of the hole and he faced her slowly. His expression was hard, his eyes wide. "We'd better go back to the Tattoo."

"Why? What's behind the wall?" she asked, frustration adding volume to her litany of questions.

"A body."

Chapter Two

"I think he's probably some poor, unfortunate homeless person who wandered into the building to escape the winter chill," Susan was saying. The woman's brown eyes were wide as she excitedly continued expounding her theory. "He must have been sick. And he probably assumed he was suffering from nothing more than a bad cold."

"I think you're letting your imagination run wild," Tory cautioned. The pout the other woman offered was at odds with her athletically lean face. Susan was a runner and it showed in her slender build. She was forever hounding Tory about the lack of physical activity in her life. Thankfully, the discovery of the skeleton had provided a diversion from Susan's usual boring reprimands on the perils of passivity.

"No," Susan insisted, looking to J.D., who gave a small nod of encouragement. "He must have crawled in through the window before succumbing to bacterial pneumonia."

"Bacterial pneumonia?" Tory echoed, feeling her eyebrows draw together.

"Sure," Susan replied. "It's very deadly if not treated. And it kills really fast."

"Well, hell," Tory said as she theatrically slapped her palm against her forehead. "The police are wasting their time investigating. Why don't you run out there and tell them what happened. It'll save the city a whole lot of time and money."

J.D. folded his arms over the back of the chair, his eyes leveled on the redhead. His expression told Tory nothing of his thoughts.

"I think your theory has a few holes in it," J.D. said.

"Really?"

"If the guy was on death's door, how do you suppose he built the wall?"

"What wall?" Susan asked.

Shrugging his shoulders, J.D. tilted his head and looked directly at Tory as he answered. "The stones that covered him aren't the same as the ones used in rest of the building. It's my guess that—"

"You can't be serious," Tory cut in. "You're suggesting that someone entombed that body in the dependency?"

"It's a real probability," he answered slowly.

"I think you've been watching too much television or something." Tory dismissed his speculation with a wave of her hand. The lingering seed of doubt wasn't as easily discharged.

His gaze didn't falter as his eyes roamed over her face. Rubbing her arms against a sudden chill, Tory shook her head, hoping to rid her mind of sudden vivid images of that nameless, faceless person meeting such a gruesome demise.

"I think you're being a bit melodramatic, J.D.," she said with forced lightness.

"Maybe," he agreed as he rose to his full height and went behind the bar.

Tory should have gone home. There was really no point in hanging around the Tattoo since the police had asked them to close down while vanloads of forensic teams scoured the area.

About an hour after the initial discovery, Shelby and Dylan Tanner arrived with their son Chad in tow. A pang of envy tugged at her heart as she watched the couple move toward her. Dylan was tall, dark and handsome; Shelby dark, exotic-looking and hugely pregnant. Dylan almost always had a tender hand on his wife—small, seemingly insignificant touches that proclaimed the extent of their deep emotional commitment to each other.

Chad was a different story. Polite people called him all-boy. He bounded into the room and immediately began pressing the buttons on the jukebox. Shelby's stern warning to stay away from the machine fell on deaf ears. Chad had a mind of his own at the tender age of eighteen months. Tory liked that.

Tory ran over and scooped the squealing child into her arms, planting kisses against his plump tummy.

"How's my favorite little man?" she asked.

"Man, man, man," was his babbled response.

"Terror is more like it," Dylan called as he draped his arm across his wife's shoulders.

"Are you a terror?" Tory asked the small boy.

He shook his head vigorously, then said, "Man."

"See?" Tory said as she shifted Chad in her arms. "He's not a terror."

"Then maybe Auntie Tory would like to take him for the weekend?" Shelby teased, a sarcastic light in her blue eyes.

"Anytime," she said earnestly. "Right, little man?"

"Man," Chad answered, nodding his dark head.

Looping his pudgy arms around her neck, Chad proceeded to give her a "skeeze." The delight in her eyes faded somewhat when she noticed J.D. leaning against the bar, a long-neck bottle of beer balanced between his thumb and forefinger. When he began to move toward them, the word *swagger* flashed across her brain. His expression was sour, distracted. Why did such an unpleasant man have to exude such sensuality? she wondered.

"You must be J.D.," Dylan said as he offered the taller man his hand.

"Guilty," J.D. responded.

"Shelby is really excited about the work you're going to do."

J.D. turned those devastating eyes on Shelby, nodding politely. "I think adding a club will allow you to draw in a younger crowd."

"That's what we're hoping," Shelby answered as she rested her head against her husband's shoulder. "And I know your mother is equally thrilled that you agreed to do the work."

"For a hefty price," Tory grumbled in a stage whisper.

Three sets of eyes turned on her. But it was the simmering hostility in J.D.'s expression that made her instantly regret the barb.

"Miss Conway thinks I'm overpriced and incapable of doing the job," J.D. explained, though his eyes never left hers.

"I'm sure that's not the case," Shelby insisted. "Tory?" she questioned. "Surely you know—"

"She knows that I prefer dramatic buildings," J.D. interrupted. "And she's right."

"Well," Tory said as she captured Chad's hand in hers to prevent his sudden fascination with the buttons of her white blouse. "I don't get a vote, now, do I, Mr. Porter? I'm nothing but a lowly waitress."

Shifting the child on her hip, Tory returned her attention to the baby. It was much easier than having to suffer the intense scrutiny of his eyes. "How about we raid the fridge?" she asked. When she got no response, she added, "Ice cream?"

"Get it," Chad answered, his fat legs bouncing with excitement.

"Not a lot," Shelby warned.

J.D. watched her disappear into the kitchen, a knot of tension forming between his shoulders.

"What was that all about?" Dylan asked.

J.D. offered a noncommittal shrug. "Miss Conway believes I'm incapable of rehabbing the building because historical sites aren't exactly part of my résumé."

"Tory believes in preserving the city," Shelby agreed. "Lord knows, she's been studying it long enough."

"She won't be studying much longer," J.D. said as he frowned. Why did he care if she'd lost her grant? He should be looking upon that bit of information as a gift from above. It could be the answer to his prayers. It was certainly a way to get Tory Conway out of his life.

"Why?" Shelby asked him.

J.D. had just finished recounting the visit by Dr. Greyson when Rose joined them. He felt the tension in his body grow worse. "So it looks like her academic career is history."

"Not if I can help it," Rose countered, patting the paperback directory.

J.D. noted a glint in his mother's eyes that instantly had him on red alert.

"That girl's entitled to her education. She's worked damned hard and I'm going to see she finishes," Rose huffed, tracing the edge of one line on her zebra-print pants.

Stifling a groan, J.D. sucked in a deep breath, then let it out slowly. "That might not be such a good idea," he suggested. He wondered if any of what he had told his mother in confidence that morning had penetrated the layers of her lacquered curls.

"Leave that to me," she told him. Her hand came out and hovered just above his arm. "I've got a plan."

"Would someone like to clue me in?" Shelby piped up, her hand moving in a circular motion over her large belly.

"Upstairs," Rose instructed.

J.D. was left alone in the dining room with Susan. He wasn't much in the mood for company, he was feeling too restless. He was starting to wonder about this trip. Perhaps it would have been easier just to have ignored Rose's request to come to South Carolina. He could have happily stayed in Florida, doing his kind of work. Rose would have remained nothing more than a name and a vague memory.

"Want me to do your palm?" Susan chirped.

"Excuse me?"

"Your palm," she repeated, glancing at his balled fist. "I sense some really intense discord in your aura."

"My aura?"

"Very telling," Susan said, her brown eyes solemn. "I can usually tell everything about a person from their aura. Yours is red."

"Red, huh?" he asked, faintly amused.

"That's bad," she insisted, genuineness dripping from each syllable. "If you let me have a look at your palm, I might be able to determine the cause of the red in your aura."

"This ought to be a kick," he mumbled as he took a seat across from her and offered his hand, palm up.

Susan bent forward and traced the lines on his hand. Her face was totally serious, as if she was completely absorbed in her examination. Her fingers were long and bony, and not nearly as soft as Tory's.

He frowned, wondering why his mind would recognize such a traitorous thought. But his subconscious wasn't finished, not by a long shot. As he sat there, he noted the many differences between the two waitresses. Susan was lanky and shapeless. Tory could only be described as voluptuous. Though he noted how hard she tried to conceal her attributes, her curvaceous body had not gone unnoticed. His frown deepened.

"I think you're about to make a life-altering decision," Susan predicted.

"Such as?"

"I'm not a fortune-teller," Susan informed him haughtily. "I can only tell you what I see, based on the physical aspects of your palm."

"Sorry." J.D. managed to sound moderately sincere.

"And see here?" She followed one of the long lines on his hand. "This is your love line. It's very long, but there's a definite interruption."

"Meaning?"

"Your love life won't be a smooth one."

Safe answer, he thought.

"But this is what concerns me," she continued, tapping her blunt nail against the edge of his hand. "These lines dissecting your life line indicate that you're in for a great deal of discord in your life. And they're all clustered together, which probably explains your bad aura."

"Come again?"

"Basically, lots of bad things will happen to you at one time. You'll experience one disaster after another."

"I can't wait," he groaned, wondering if this trip to South Carolina would prove to be the catalyst for this "disturbance of his aura."

"But there's hope," Susan said brightly. "Once you get past that stuff, you should be very content with your life."

"Great," he mused aloud. "I'll keep that in mind whenever my life starts going to hell."

Susan's dark eyes met his. "As for your aura, I think you might want to try some deep-breathing exercises. Relaxation techniques are quite effective in achieving a color change. You might even make it all the way to yellow."

"There's a goal," he whispered as he gently pulled his hand away. "Thanks for the insights."

"Anytime," Susan answered. Grabbing her over-size nylon knapsack, the woman slung it over her thin shoulder as she got to her feet. "Practice that breathing," she called out as she left.

He took a long pull on his beer and savored the bitterness as it went down. This was certainly one of the more interesting days in his life. He'd discovered a skeleton and had had his palm and aura analyzed. He began to chuckle.

"Something funny?"

Tory approached him with something akin to trepidation in her eyes.

"Susan just checked out my aura and my palm."

His explanation erased the caution from her expression. Her half smile had a disturbing effect on him.

"Don't let her hear you laugh," he warned. "She takes that stuff seriously. I made that mistake when she warned me of impending doom."

"Really? And what did our little soothsayer tell you?"

His eyes drifted to her shapely backside as she slipped behind the bar and filled a glass with soda.

"She's convinced I'm about to have a life-altering experience. Something about too many intersections in my life line."

J.D. felt his mouth curve in a wide smile. "It would seem that Susan is a one-trick pony," Tory said.

"Why's that?"

"That's basically the same story she handed me."

She stood next to the table, but made no move to join him. She brought the glass to her lips. It was the first time he'd really looked at her mouth. He guessed it would be soft.

"Want to join me?"

"No," she answered quickly.

Too quickly, he thought.

"They were just placing that disgusting thing on a stretcher when I gave Chad back to Shelby."

"He's a cute kid."

His observation was greeted by a surprised look.

"Yes," she agreed. "Chad's adorable."

"So." He paused long enough to take another swallow. "How come you're hanging around?"

"I'm just waiting for the police to finish," she told him. "They've got my car blocked in."

"You could ask them to move it."

"I could, but I don't mind waiting."

"Patience is a virtue."

He could almost hear her spine stiffen.

"Why do you feel the need to mock me?" she asked pointedly.

"I wasn't mocking. Simply making an observation."

"Miss?"

Tory turned in answer to the male voice. One of the detectives marched forward, his badge dangling from the breast pocket of his tan suit jacket.

"Would it be possible for me to get a glass of water?"

"Sure," Tory answered as she slipped behind the bar and filled a glass with ice.

"J. D. Porter," he said, extending his hand to the man.

"Greer," the detective responded, wiping his hand on his slacks before engaging in the handshake. "You're Rose's..."

"Son," J.D. answered without inflection.

The detective regarded him briefly before Tory appeared with the glass. "Thanks," he said. "It's hot as all get-out today."

"Have they taken the body away?" Tory asked.

"What was left of him."

"Then it was a man?" J.D. asked.

"We're pretty sure, based on the size and shape of the pelvic bones."

"Any idea who he was?"

"Not a clue," Greer answered. "But the lab boys think he's been here a while. Some medical mumbo jumbo about the condition and density of the bone."

"How creepy," Tory groaned. "I can't tell you how many times I've been near that building in the five years I've been working here."

"That long?" Greer asked, immediately putting down his glass and feeling for his pad and pen.

"Yes, sir," J.D. heard her answer. "I worked for the previous owner—Mr. Brewster."

"Didn't your family use to own this place before Brewster?" J.D. queried.

Tory shot him a quick glance of annoyance, then turned her attention back to the detective. "My father owned this place until about fifteen years ago."

"Do you know where I can find Brewster?" Greer asked.

"He died," Tory answered.

"How about your father?"

"I'm afraid you won't have any luck there, either."

"He's deceased?" Greer asked.

J.D. watched as she lowered her eyes.

"He left town."

"Do you have an address?"

"I haven't heard from him," she answered in a small voice.

J.D. felt a small stab of compassion for the woman. He knew all too well what it was like to have a parent suddenly disappear from your life. He placed his hand on her shoulder. She shrugged away from his touch.

"My father left us when I was ten. We never heard from him."

"Sorry," Greer mumbled as he flipped the notebook closed. "I guess there's—"

"Detective?"

An obviously excited man dressed in a wilted uniform rushed into the room. A plastic bag dangled from his dirt-smudged hand.

"What have you got?" Greer asked as he cupped his hand beneath the item in the evidence bag.

"We found this in the soil after they moved the remains."

J.D. moved closer, as did Tory. The item caught and reflected the light. "A ring," Greer mumbled.

"Has initials, too," the officer chimed excitedly.

"R.C.," Greer read.

J.D. watched the horror fill Tory's wide eyes. Her mouth opened for a scream that never materialized. She simply went limp, falling right into his outstretched arms. His handsome features grew faint and fuzzy, until she could no longer hold on to his image.

Chapter Three

His eyes opened reluctantly, followed almost immediately by a telltale stab of pain in his lower back. Using his legs for leverage, J.D. hoisted his stiff frame to a sitting position. Rubbing the stubble on his chin, he squinted against the harsh rays of morning light spilling over a faded set of clashing curtains. Holding his breath, he listened for sound. Nothing.

He found a clock on the kitchen wall. Well, he decided, as he began a burglar-quiet search of the cabinets, it wasn't really much of a kitchen. Hell, he added, feeling the frown on his lips, it wasn't really much of an apartment.

Leaning against the counter, he surveyed the single room, feeling his stomach lurch in protest to the stark surroundings. Tory Conway appeared to be living one step above poverty. For some unknown reason, that rankled.

The single-serving coffeepot gurgled behind him. In the center of the room there was a card table with two mismatched chairs, their seats little more than shredded strips of faded vinyl. The computer sitting on top of the table was antiquated, probably five years removed from the sleek electronic notebook he had so casually brought along from Miami. The first stir-rings of guilt did little to improve his mood.

He found a coffee cup on the drain board and actually smiled when he realized it was from the Rose Tattoo. A quick check of the drawers indicated that the utensils and most of the other items were also from his mother's restaurant.

Mother. His grimace returned with a vengeance. What in hell had he gotten himself into? he wondered as he poured the coffee and took a sip. The liquid scalded his mouth. Why had he listened to Wesley? This little exercise in closure had turned into an un-mitigated disaster. He wasn't a preservationist. He was an architect. And a damned good one. No matter what the sassy little blonde sleeping in the other room thought.

Stifling the groan that rose in his throat, J.D. returned to the lumpy sofa, which had served as his bed, and grabbed the telephone. Pounding the keypad, he cradled the receiver against his chin as he took another sip of the too strong coffee.

"Hello?"

"Wes, it's me."

"Big brother?" came the groggy reply. "Do you realize what time it is?"

He hadn't realized, but he didn't feel the inclination to apologize. "Early."

"No sh—"

"I've got a problem."

He could hear the rustle of bed covers, and he could easily envision his brother groping on the nightstand for his round, metal-framed glasses. Wesley was one of those people who couldn't hear without his glasses.

"You and mother aren't relating well?"

That I-just-got-my-degree-in-psychiatry, inflection-free voice was enough to make J.D. grit his teeth. He was beginning to think Wes's budding medical career was going to be a stiff pain in his rump.

"We aren't relating at all," he answered flatly. "But that isn't the problem."

"How can that not be a problem?" Wes countered.

"Because I have a more pressing problem with a body."

"Oh." Wesley snickered. "And is this body a blonde, brunette or redhead?"

"I'm serious," J.D. insisted. "It's a dead body. Deceased. Not living."

"She was married and you did something rash?"

"Good Lord, Wes! I thought psychiatrists were supposed to be good listeners. You're not hearing me."

"You're serious?" his brother asked, his tone indicating he had finally grasped the situation.

"Hell, yes," J.D. answered, raking his hand through his hair. "And it looks like the body might be the father of the girl I told you about."

"Woman."

"What?"

He heard his brother expel one of those condescendingly patient breaths. "The person you described was a woman, not a girl. We're talking about Victoria Conway, right?"

"Right."

"The one with pretty blue eyes, an incredible mouth and boobs that—"

"Yes," he growled.

"Hey," Wesley continued. "You're the one who told me you were astounded she didn't fall facedown from the weight of those hooters."

"Thank you," J.D. managed to say tightly. "Forget what I said before. Fact is, the body I found might just turn out to be her father."

He heard a low whistle before Wesley said, "Gonna be kind of tough to shaft the lady when she's in the midst of burying Daddy, isn't it."

"No kidding," J.D. admitted. "And I wasn't going to shaft her. I was thinking more along the lines of a nice, quiet buyout."

"Think she'll be interested in doing business with a man who originally judged her by her bra size?"

"Wesley," J.D. said from between clenched teeth. "I called for your advice, not a lecture."

"Then you shouldn't have confided all your observations about the lady's physical attributes."

"Brothers are supposed to confide things like that. It's part of the male-bonding process."

Wesley's laugh was low and easy. It served as a vivid reminder to J.D. of their inherent differences.

"Careful, big brother. That sounded dangerously like an introspective moment. Not your usual style."

"Finding skeletons in walls isn't par for the course, either."

"I don't know," Wesley began arbitrarily. "If you're willing to come to grips with the skeletons in your closet, one more in the wall should be no sweat."

"You aren't helping."

"What would you suggest I do?"

"Get your butt up here."

"In good time," Wesley announced. "That was the deal."

"But things have changed since we struck that bargain," J.D. said on a breath.

"And you can roll with the punches," Wesley said easily. "I think this may turn out to be a very healthy experience for you."

"Right," J.D. grumbled. His coffee had gone cold and it left a bitter taste in his mouth as he forced himself to swallow. "If you came up here, you could deal with the girl. She needs someone like you."

"That's not what you said the other evening," Wesley countered. "You indicated that one night in your capable arms would have her eating out of your hand."

"I was wrong," J.D. admitted. Hearing his own arrogant words made him squirm uncomfortably in his seat. "She's not what I thought at first."

"Wouldn't let you in her pants, huh?"

"Not a chance."

OPENING HER EYES, Tory blinked against the confusion clouding her lagging brain. Her hand ran over the surface of the rumpled comforter. The movement caused her to feel the coolness of the sheets against her skin. *Too much skin,* she thought as she threw the bedspread toward her feet. "What?" she mumbled as she discovered she was wearing nothing but her bra and panties. The flame red garments stood out against the stark white sheets. With wide eyes, she allowed her gaze to dart around the room as she tried to pry memories from her brain.

Her fingers feathered her bangs as she concentrated. Recall came slowly. Pain, followed by so many emotions that she lost count. Her father was dead.

Had been all these years. A small groan escaped her slightly parted lips.

Images from childhood mingled with bits and pieces of the scene she had waged in the Tattoo. Images of her parents, recalled through the eyes of a mere child. Images of being in J.D.'s arms, remembered by a lingering heat on her skin.

Tory stood on wobbly legs. Only then did she recollect Rose forcing several pills down her throat last night. At least she thought it was last night. Everything seemed to be trapped in a haze. Grabbing her short robe off the hook, she tugged it over her shoulders and yanked open the door. Her eyes collided with a set of gray ones.

"What...?" She managed to tear the word from her constricted throat.

"Good morning," he said easily, unfolding himself from the sofa.

Her mouth remained open as she took in the scene. J.D. had a tousled, rugged look that cemented her to the spot. His dark hair was mussed, as if someone had been running their fingers through it. His shirt was open, and the edges pulled farther apart as he rose to his full height of well over six feet. Tory's eyes fell to the thick, black curls and then lower, where they tapered and disappeared beneath the waistband of his jeans.

Realizing too late that such a brazen appraisal might prove dangerous, she lifted her gaze to his. His expression was intense, his eyes narrowed to a glistening silver. Again she realized the error of her ways too late. She could feel his eyes as they took in the lacy edges of her bra, could feel them linger at the valley between her breasts.

Feeling her skin color the same deep red as her lingerie, Tory grabbed the edges of her belt, twisting her exposed body away from the scrutiny of his examination. She'd given him an eyeful, she thought ruefully as she tied the belt so tightly that it actually made each breath painful.

"I made another pot of coffee," he told her, his voice deep and as smooth as smoke.

"Thanks," she said, willing herself into composure. "What are you doing here?" she asked as she padded into the kitchen. The vision of his eyes followed, narrowed with interest and a purely dangerous glint.

"Rose didn't think you should be alone."

"So she left you here with me?"

Tory turned to find that his expression had changed. His eyes were still narrowed, but she saw flashes of barely leashed anger that stilled her stiff movements.

"Any reason Rose wouldn't trust us together?" he asked, one dark eyebrow arched high.

"We aren't exactly close," she offered, hoping her voice sounded more calm than she actually felt.

"Not because I haven't tried," he returned as a lazy half smile curved one corner of his mouth.

Tory directed a heavy sigh toward her bangs. "Don't start, J.D."

He moved with a quickness and grace that belied his size. Suddenly he was in front of her, his broad, bare chest dominating her vision. "Believe me, doll," he began in a low hum, "when I start on you, you'll know it."

His words burned against her ears and she fought the instinct to raise a hand and slap his arrogant face. But she decided to stand her ground. She would not react. It was, she had learned, her only weapon against this man's blatant maleness. "Well," she said, clearing her throat on the word. "As you can see, I'm fine, so you can just go crawl back under your rock."

She smiled up at him, fighting the constriction in her throat when she looked at him through the thickness of her lashes. J.D. didn't move. Not at all. He simply allowed his body to heat the air between them. Forced her to breathe in the scent of his skin. Power fairly radiated from this man. Power that Tory was only beginning to comprehend. One thing she knew, she realized as she struggled to hold his gaze, J. D. Porter was way out of her league. She surrendered, closing her eyes before lowering her chin fractionally.

"Thank you for staying," she said after a drawn-out silence, punctuated only by the even sound of his breathing. Perhaps graciousness might accomplish her goal of dismissing this disturbing man.

"No problem," he said as he slowly stepped back. The edge to his voice was still there, but it wasn't quite as sharp.

Tory turned back to the sink, thinking how helpful it might be to douse herself with cold water. J.D. somehow managed to ignite small fires in every cell of her body. She reached up into the cabinet in search of a coffee cup. His sharp intake of breath was as thrilling as it was disquieting. It didn't take a rocket scientist to realize that the action, however innocent, had resulted in her flashing the big man a goodly amount of leg. She lowered her arm slowly, snidely hoping to give him a healthy dose of his own medicine.

With a cup of coffee in hand, she finally mustered the nerve to look at him again. The flash of anger was gone, all right, but it had been replaced by something even more devastating. Hunger—raw, passionate and definitely frightening. A small voice of reason chanted that saying about playing with fire as she bolted for the living room.

J.D. followed, his pace slow, but determined. It conjured visions of a predator stalking its prey. Tory wasn't at all sure she could handle being this man's quarry.

"Rose called earlier," he said conversationally.

His calm, businesslike demeanor only made her more aware of her own raging pulse. The man was obviously some sort of machine. She'd seen him do this time and time again during the course of their short acquaintance. J.D. could be in a rage one minute, calm as a gentle breeze the next.

"I should call and apologize," Tory said, tracing the top of her cup with her fingernail.

"For what?"

"Falling apart yesterday."

"Appropriate under the circumstances," he said as he turned one of her metal chairs and mounted it. His well-developed forearms rested against its back.

Her interest fell to his exposed stomach, wondering absently how those ripples of muscle would feel beneath her fingertips.

"Don't you think?"

"Sorry," Tory mumbled as her attention dropped to study a polyurethaned knot in the wooden floor.

"I said, I thought your actions were appropriate under the circumstances. That must have been quite a shock for you."

"It was," she admitted softly. "I still can't believe he's been there all this time."

"Where did you think he was?"

Sitting at the table and tucking her bare feet under the hem of her short robe, Tory placed the coffee cup on the table. "I just always believed he'd suffered some sort of midlife crisis and bolted."

"Leaving his loving wife and daughter behind?"

Tory peered up at him through her lashes, trying to gauge his sincerity. Unfortunately, J.D. had the perfect face for poker. It revealed absolutely nothing.

Her lids fluttered closed as she felt a swell of emotion grip her chest. "I can't tell you how much I've hated him all these years. How many times I've wished him dead for what he did to my mother."

"You didn't know."

Somehow his words failed to bring absolution.

"Mother," she said, her eyes open and straining against her tight lids. "I've got to go out to Ashley Villas."

"Where?"

"My mother's home," she said by way of explanation.

Tory deposited her coffee cup and turned toward the bedroom in a flurry of activity. It took several seconds for her brain to register the fact that J.D. hadn't moved a blessed muscle.

"I don't mean to be antisocial, Mr. Porter," she said stiffly, "but I've got to go see my mother. Tell her . . ."

Nodding, J.D. rose and began buttoning his shirt. Tory refused to look, no matter how much she might want to.

"How long will it take you to get ready?"

"How long?" she gasped.

"Minutes? Hours? How long?"

"Why?"

"Because I need to know how soon to pick you up."

"Why would you pick me up?"

"Because your car is still at the Rose Tattoo."

"So," she said, her voice faltering slightly. "I can grab the bus and pick it up."

"No, you can't." J.D. dug into the front pocket of his jeans. Instantly she recognized her key ring as it dangled from his forefinger.

"Give me my keys," she instructed, annoyance stiffening her spine.

"Can't," he drawled with an exaggerated sigh.

"Can't or won't?"

"Can't," he insisted, pretending to be hurt by her insinuation. "The doctor said you weren't to drive for twenty-four hours after taking those pills."

"Then I'll make other arrangements," she told him with a wave of her hand.

"Seems kind of stupid since I'm ready and able."

But for what, exactly? her brain screamed. "I don't think—"

"No thought required," he said as he tossed her keys in the air, captured them in his big palm, then slipped them back into his pocket. "I'll be back in about forty-five minutes."

THE PURPOSE FOR the cold shower was twofold. First, J.D. hoped it might revive his sleep-deprived senses. But, more important, he was trying to cleanse the memory of her voluptuous body from his mind. Closing his eyes against the spray, his mind immediately brought forth the image of her pale skin... and the slope of her full breasts spilling over the lacy top of her bra. He didn't have to touch the garment to know it was silk—like her skin. The vivid red lingerie set against her creamy skin reminded him of a ripe, red berry atop a snowdrift.

"God," he groaned, earning himself a mouthful of cool, chlorine-scented water. He'd been too long without a woman. That was the only explanation for his body's rigid and painful response to Tory.

He stepped from the shower, grabbed a towel and blotted the water from his skin. Droplets of water fell from his hair as he grabbed his razor. He was glad for a task that required his full attention.

J.D. vigorously towel dried his hair as he stepped into the master suite of his condo. Guilt tugged at his conscience as he paused to look at his surroundings. A king-size white rattan bed dominated the large space, with no fewer than three chests of drawers. There was a desk in the corner, his laptop lay open on it, gathering dust. His condo also included a living room, dining area and a kitchen that could have swallowed Tory's entire apartment. His intellect reminded him that he'd had no way of knowing she would be a person of such modest means. But that knowledge didn't seem to stem the surge of guilt as he tossed the towel into a pile of laundry that would be handled by the cleaning woman.

Selecting a fresh pair of jeans and a thin cotton shirt, J.D. tucked his wallet and keys into his pants pockets and took the stairs to the parking lot two at a time. He was greeted by a slap of humid air that barely fazed his well-conditioned body. The air in the red interior of his white Mercedes was stale before he flipped on the air-conditioning. He turned out into the midday traffic and tapped a disk into the CD player as he drove.

Ashley Villas. He repeated her words in his brain. It sounded like one of those golf and tennis communities that lined the southeastern seaboard like smooth shells. He tried to develop a mental image of Tory's mother. The woman would probably be in her fifties and have a strong personality. He guessed she would be small, like her daughter, but more athletic than soft. Her skin would be wrinkled and weathered from too many trips around the back nine and not enough sunscreen. He grimaced, envisioning a brash woman wearing a white golf skirt and those funny little socks with the fuzzy little pastel balls that stuck out the back of her shoes. She was probably fiercely competitive. Tory was a fighter, that much he knew. That attribute was normally learned at home.

He frowned, suddenly realizing his thoughts were more suited to his inquisitive younger brother. Wesley was into analysis, not him.

Her apartment didn't look much better in the light of day. It looked exactly like what it was—a garage converted into barely livable space.

She came through the door before he had an opportunity to kill the engine. Her dress forced a small smile to his lips. It fell far short of flattering, he mused as he watched her move toward him. It basically covered her from her throat to her ankles, a swirl of gauzy beige fabric designed specifically *not* to cling to her in any of the right places. His eyes fell to where her breasts strained against the material. He wondered if beneath that shapeless, colorless dress, she wore those wispy, sexy undergarments. His body responded uncomfortably to his imagination.

"You're punctual," she said as she slid in beside him.

"A regular Boy Scout," he grumbled.

"Boy Scouts aren't surly, as a rule," she told him as she folded her delicate hands in her lap.

"Have much experience with Boy Scouts, do you?"

"Probably as much as you do."

"I'll have you know I almost made it to Eagle Scout," he informed her, his chest puffed out slightly.

"Almost doesn't count."

His chest deflated. "I suppose not," he acknowledged reluctantly. "Which way?"

"Take the Mark Clark." She pointed north.

The expressway was crowded with minivans and trucks sporting business logos. But his attention was on the woman to his right. "You can relax, I won't bite."

"I am relaxed."

"You don't look it."

"How can I not be relaxed? Sitting in this car is like sitting in your living room."

"Not *your* living room, doll," he promised her with a sidelong glance. "I slept on what you've got passing for a couch."

"It serves its purpose," she said with a shrug of her shoulders.

That small movement filled the interior of the car with the distinctive scent of gardenia. His mind immediately demanded to know if it was her soap, her shampoo or her cologne. Would he be able to taste it on her skin? Would he be able to keep his mind on the road long enough to prevent a ten-car pileup?

J.D. decided to concentrate on making polite conversation. "Did you call your mother to let her know you were coming?"

"It isn't necessary."

He sensed a tension in her voice that piqued his interest. "You two that close?"

"I love my mother."

He realized instantly that she hadn't actually answered his question. This from the woman who had not bothered to spare her tongue when it came to his strained relationship with Rose.

"Do you think she saw the newspaper?" he asked, nodding to the folded copy lying on the seat between them.

"No."

"She's not a reader?"

"No."

"How do you think she'll take the news about your father?"

"Calmly."

His only hint that she wasn't quite as composed as her limited answers implied was the sight of her hand as she played with the strands of wheat-colored hair sculpted around her slender throat. The tremor in her fingers was undeniable.

"You tense?"

"Tense?"

"Nervous? Agitated? Upset?"

She didn't answer right away. He glanced over once, only to have his eyes fall on the gentle rise and fall of her chest as she breathed deeply through her slightly parted lips.

"I'm just not sure how Mama will handle the news."

J.D. gripped the wheel a bit more tightly. "Her long-lost husband is dead. If she loved him, I'm sure she'll be devastated."

"What do you mean 'if she loved him'?" Tory fairly shouted at him.

He saw the spark in her ice blue eyes and was glad to see some of the life come back to her.

"Sorry," he mumbled, lifting his hands off the wheel in a brief gesture of mock surrender. "I just meant that it's been, what? Fifteen years? Love and memories fade."

She turned her head so that he could no longer get a fix on her expression.

"How about you?"

"How about I what?" she answered dully.

"How are you holding up?"

"Are you asking me if I read the newspaper article?" Tory asked, gesturing toward the paper between them.

"Yes." He realized he was holding his breath, not certain why he had suddenly broached this potentially dangerous subject.

"I don't believe everything I read in the papers."

"Smart approach."

"But," she said as she turned, "if the police are correct in their early assessment of the case, my father didn't desert me. He was murdered."

"They weren't clear on that point," J.D. told her.

"One of them stated that there appeared to be a bullet wound in the skull—"

"But that they needed to run tests."

She scooted closer to the door, as if she wanted as much distance between them as possible.

"I must admit, Tory," he began in a deliberately soft, nonthreatening tone, "I'm astounded by your composure. If someone told me my father might have been murdered, I think I'd go ballistic."

"As strange as this may sound, hearing their theory made me feel strangely comforted."

"How so?"

"Because it means he didn't choose to walk out of my life. It means he didn't leave me."

J.D. hated the effect her soft, almost choked, words were having on his gut. Feeling compassion for this woman was dangerous.

"Turn here," she said as they approached an exit.

Silently, J.D. followed her instructions for the next several miles. The landscape was little more than swampy grasses and clusters of evergreens. Hardly an ideal sight for a golf and tennis community.

His eyes fixed on a wooden sign about a hundred yards down the road. It swayed gently on the currents of the passing cars, but he could still make out the bold, black print.

"Ashley Villas Convalescent Center?" he read aloud as he pulled into the lot, threw the car into park and killed the engine.

"None other," she responded, her voice cracking with emotion.

"Your mother lives in a convalescent center?" he asked.

"Yes," she answered as she opened the door and stepped from the car.

Grabbing the folded newspaper, J.D. tucked it under his arm and then jogged to catch up to her. "You could have said something."

"I did," she responded without looking at him. "I told you I would have preferred coming alone."

He inclined his head in respect as he held open one of the center's shining glass doors.

"Tory!" a male voice bellowed down the otherwise silent corridor. Tory smiled wanely at the dark-haired man sauntering toward her. "I should have guessed I'd run into you here today. Tough thing about your dad."

He watched as she accepted the huge hand from the man he guessed to be about fifty, though his physique belied his age. His clothes told J.D. two things—first, the guy definitely had bucks; and second, he dressed for the sole purpose of attracting women.

"Cal Matthews," she said, almost as an afterthought, "This is J.D. Porter."

The two men shook hands.

Tory continued, "Cal used to work for my dad."

"Sorry I can't stay," Cal cut in, making a point of looking at the Rolex on his wrist, "but you know how it is."

Tory nodded. J.D. wanted to question her about the guy, when a plump nurse approached

"Poor child," the large woman with skin the color of chocolate came shuffling forward, her arms held open.

"Hello, Gladys," she answered before being enfolded in the woman's ample bosom.

Gladys gave him a once-over that made J.D. feel as if he were back in Sunday school. He didn't think he'd passed inspection, either—not judging from the wary look on the nurse's round face.

"I read all about what happened in the paper," Gladys said, crooking Tory beneath her arm in a purely protective fashion. Her dark eyes continued to assess J.D. "And who is this young man?"

"J.D. Porter," Tory said. "He's in Charleston visiting Rose."

"You told me about him," Gladys said with a thoughtful nod. "This is the man who's going to ruin the Tattoo?"

"The same," Tory admitted without so much as a trace of apology in her expression. "J.D., this is Gladys Halloday, R.N."

"I prefer to think of my work as improving the property," J.D. corrected as he offered his hand to the rather imposing woman.

"Change can be good," Gladys said with a nod of her graying head.

Arms locked, the two women began to move down the hall. J.D. followed, feeling much like an intruder.

The place reminded him more of a hotel than a nursing home. There was no ammonia smell, no hiss of oxygen tanks. The place had carpeting and wall-paper, comfortable chairs and a bulletin board full of scheduled activities.

"There's Dr. Trimble. He's been waiting for you," he heard Gladys say. "He spent a lot of time with your mama this morning."

J.D. saw a paternalistic look appear in the doctor's eyes when the man spotted them moving down the hall. It was becoming obvious to J.D. that Tory was a frequent and popular visitor here.

The doctor uttered words of condolence and didn't bother giving J.D. a second glance. His face was a palette of concerned lines as he took both of Tory's hands in his.

"I'm afraid I didn't get any reaction when I told her about Robert."

"None?"

He watched as the doctor's expression grew sad. "I'm sorry, Tory. There was nothing."

"I'd like to see her now." Tory glanced over her shoulder but didn't quite meet J.D.'s eyes. "Alone," she added.

Gladys planted herself in the center of the hallway, her expression all but daring him to try to push past her. J.D. wasn't about to take on the nurse. He'd learned a long time ago when to back down from confrontation. And this was definitely one of those times. He watched Tory disappear into the last room on the right.

For the next forty minutes, he sat in a small lounge under the watchful eye of his self-appointed guard. J.D. thumbed through the paper, wondering what Tory and her mother were discussing. *No reaction at all.* The words filtered back through his brain. He finished reading the paper and piled it on the seat next to him. He looked up to find Gladys away from her post.

Feeling restless and a bit intrigued, J.D. got up, telling himself that he was only going to walk far enough to stretch the cramped muscles of his legs.

His walk took him past the lookout station, down to the last door on the right. The door was ajar and he gave a soft push, widening the crack.

He was shocked by what he saw. At first glance, he could have been looking at a child, she was so tiny. Then he saw her face. Tory's mother couldn't have weighed more than eighty pounds. The white sheets nearly swallowed her frail, limp body. But it wasn't her size as much as her face that forced him to suck in a breath. She looked barely older than her daughter. Her pale skin was smooth, nearly devoid of lines. The difference was in the eyes. The woman in bed stared blankly into space, apparently untouched by the things and people around her.

"You would have laughed, Mama." He heard Tory's voice and followed it. She was framed by the light from the window, her back to him. "You remember when I was ten and I started to develop? That nasty David Coultraine paid two of his friends to hold my arms while he peeked down my blouse? And I screamed that I'd hate all boys until my dying day?"

She paused, as if awaiting a response that never came.

"After I stopped crying, you told me one day I'd be swooning over boys. Well, you should have seen me last night. I fell right into a man's waiting arms, just like you said."

J.D. nearly jumped back when she turned and moved to the bed, sitting on, but barely rumpling, the neatly tucked bed coverings. The woman didn't move, he noted. She gave no indication that she was even aware that her beautiful daughter sat at her side. J.D. swallowed the lump of emotion in his throat.

"The doctor said he told you about Daddy," Tory said as she continued her monologue. The pauses, he quickly realized, were the result of a long history of these one-sided conversations.

Tory lifted the woman's limp hand. Something glittered in the light. J.D. moved closer to pull the object into focus. It was a ring, a copy of the one that the cops had found with the skeleton. From its placement on the lifeless hand, he guessed it was her wedding band.

"He didn't leave us, Mama. No matter what else, he didn't run off."

Tory took the hand to her face and forced it along the side of her cheek, simulating a loving, motherly stroke.

"That day after he left," Tory began, her voice dropping to a hard-to-hear whisper, "you told me he wasn't coming back. You sat me on top of the bar and told me that."

J.D. could easily imagine the scene. He felt it in the twisted knot of his stomach.

"Please, Mama," she begged, holding the hand to her heart. "Please tell me you didn't kill him."

Chapter Four

J.D. backed out of the doorway slowly, soundlessly pulling on the door as he made his exit.

Confusion caused deep lines of concentration to tug at the corners of his mouth. Glancing down the corridor, he spotted Dr. Trimble flipping through a chart near the nurse's station. J.D. reached him in three purposeful strides.

"Dr. Trimble?"

The man peered at him over the top of his half glasses. His graying eyebrows thinned above his clear brown eyes.

"I'm J. D. Porter," he said, offering his hand. "I came with Tory."

The doctor nodded, apparently approving on some unspoken level. "Nice of you to come along. I'm sure today has been particularly difficult for her."

"Yes," J.D. agreed quickly.

"Of course, she'd never admit it," Trimble added with a wry smile. "But I'm sure you already know that about her."

"Sir?"

"She has this incredible capacity for only focusing on the positive. Heaven help her if she ever loses that defense mechanism."

J.D. stifled a groan. This guy sounded exactly like his brother. Why the hell couldn't they just say it in plain English? he wondered.

"About her mother," J.D. began.

The doctor nodded, making him wonder if the gesture was some sort of technique taught in medical school. Wesley nodded a lot, too.

"Mrs. Conway didn't respond when she was informed of her husband's fate," Dr. Trimble said.

"Stroke?"

The doctor's eyebrows drew together and he regarded J.D. with sudden interest. "Tory hasn't explained her mother's illness?"

J.D. shook his head. "You know Tory," he said with a shrug.

His seemingly innocent remark appeared to relax the other man. "I suppose it's still quite difficult for her to verbalize her feelings."

"Very," J.D. agreed.

"I've suggested counseling on several occasions," he said as he placed the chart on the counter and pulled the glasses off the bridge of his nose. "Especially after her grandmother died. I felt, and still feel, that Tory is unwilling to accept the finality of her mother's condition."

"Cancer?" J.D. said.

The doctor smiled sadly. "Nothing quite so socially acceptable, Mr. Porter."

"AIDS?"

The doctor's laugh was even sadder than his smile. "Tory's mother has suffered a complete and total personality break. It is my opinion that she will never recover.''

"Personality break?"

"Nervous breakdown times ten," Dr. Trimble explained. "She hasn't moved or spoken for almost fifteen years."

"Sweet Jesus," J.D. uttered between clenched teeth.

"I don't think Jesus will listen if you speak to Him in that tone," a familiar female voice said.

J.D. spun on the heels of his boots, feeling his face burn under the accusation in Tory's eyes.

"I wasn't trying to pry."

"Not much."

"I think it might be good for you to share your confidences with your friend," Dr. Trimble told her.

"I'll keep that in mind the next time I'm in the company of a friend."

J.D. heard the shuffling of paper behind him as the doctor continued. "I know this is probably an awkward time, Tory, but you need to contact the business office on your next visit."

J.D. watched what little color there was drain from her face. Her thick lashes fluttered before her eyes closed tightly. Without making a sound, she sucked in several deep breaths and nodded to the doctor.

"I'm ready to leave," she informed him in a frosty tone.

J.D. followed her from the building, knowing he should apologize, but unable to find the appropriate words. No more grant; no more father; and the next worst thing to no mother. The reality of her life pierced some private part of his heart. He unlocked the car door for her and held it open.

"I forgot my paper," he said just as he slammed the door.

He disappeared into the building and came back ten minutes later with the paper tucked beneath his arm.

"I could have suffocated in here," she told him when he slid behind the wheel. "If I were a dog, you might have thought to leave the window open a crack."

"If you were a dog," he told her as his finger flicked the underside of her chin, "you'd be better trained."

TWO WEEKS AFTER the discovery of the body, Tory was dutifully back waiting tables at the Rose Tattoo. It was Friday, she thought with a resigned sigh. Payday for most folks, which usually meant decent tips for her. The week she'd taken off had cost her dearly. She'd be pulling double shifts for the rest of the month just to meet her bills. Forget luxuries like food.

"Evening, girlie."

"Hi, Grif," she said, smiling at the old man's watery blue eyes. "The usual?"

"And keep 'em coming."

Sliding a napkin in front of him, she tugged the pencil from behind her ear and made a note on her pad. Grif—short for Cliff Griffen—had occupied that particular table every Friday and Saturday night for nearly twenty years. Tory liked him—liked the comfort his continuity brought.

Placing her tray on the side bar, she waited until Josh the bartender sauntered over, towel draped over one shoulder.

She said, "Dewars and water—"

"Easy on the water," they said in unison.

"How is old Grif this evening?"

"Fine," Tory answered just before popping an olive in her mouth.

"You aren't supposed to do that," Josh chided. "They're for paying customers."

Good-naturedly, she stuck out her tongue, careful to hide the gesture as she moved off, drink balanced in the center of her tray.

"Miss?"

"Be right there," she promised the man before depositing the drink in front of Grif.

Quickly, she retraced her steps. "Yes, sir?"

"Our food?" he demanded in a huff.

"I'll go check," she said, offering a smile.

"We have theater tickets," he announced, as if that alone would charbroil the salmon fillets faster.

"I'll see what I can do."

She went directly to the kitchen, hoping the hostility she sensed from "Mr. Theater Tickets" wasn't going to set the tone for the evening.

"My dinners?" she called to the chef.

He looked up from his grill and said, "Almost ready."

Snagging a halved cherry tomato and popping it in her mouth, she got up on her toes and looked out into the dining room. "Theater Tickets" looked restless.

"C'mon, Mickey," she yelled. "Customer's waiting."

Clutching her tray, Tory felt an odd tingling at the base of her spine. She turned slowly and saw him lingering in the doorway.

His dark head was tilted to one side, shrouding his eyes with a disturbing shadow.

"Miss Conway," he drawled as he pushed himself away from the doorjamb.

"Mr. Porter," she returned with false friendliness. She surveyed his clothing and added, "I didn't know they made silk paisley ties in clip-on."

His laughter was deep and the sound circled her like a caress. "Mind that sharp tongue, doll. You might cut yourself."

"Sorry to disappoint you," she said sweetly, "but I've got more important fish to serve."

"I think you mean fry."

For once in her life, her timing was perfect. No sooner had the words left his mouth than Mickey placed the plates of grilled fish up on the serving counter. Placing them on the tray, Tory escaped the heat of the kitchen, trying not to notice the smoldering gray eyes that bore into her back.

Over the next several hours, Tory didn't have time to think, let alone to wonder where J.D. was hiding. The pockets of her apron began to fill to a comfortable level of tips at about the same time her feet gave out. She was bone-tired and filled with relief when the crowd thinned to just a single couple and Grif, who sat nursing his fourth drink as he watched out the window.

"Need another?" she asked cheerfully as she leaned against his table.

"Not tonight," he said in that raspy voice that spoke of too many cigarettes. "I'm going hunting in the morning. Ever hunt with a hangover?"

"Can't say as I have," Tory answered with a laugh. She patted the back of his callused hand, her fingers brushing the gaudy gold band on his pudgy pinkie. "I'll ring you out." She often wondered why he wore that awful ring when his clothing fairly screamed aging yachtsman.

Susan was perched on one of the bar stools, counting her tips. Tory smiled as she watched the methodical way her mystical friend placed all the bills in the same direction, matching the edges on all four sides. Susan's reverence for all things metaphysical was surpassed only by her reverence for all things monetary.

"Have a good night?" Tory queried as she ran a check through the register.

"I had a walk-out," Susan complained. "They stuck me with two rounds of shooters with beer chasers. I hate frat boys. No class."

"No argument," Tory said with feeling.

She gave Grif and the couple at her other table their checks and waited to collect their money.

Rolling her head around her stiff shoulders, Tory stood on one foot and cleared her throat. The bartender managed to drag himself away from a swaying redhead to strut to her end of the bar. "Could you ring these two before you play your nightly game of roulette?"

"I'm careful, Tory."

"The CDC would probably beg to differ," she countered, some of the teasing gone from her voice. "They would classify you as engaging in dangerous behavior."

"Don't knock it 'til you've tried it," he retorted. "I'll be happy to keep tomorrow night open for you."

"She's busy tomorrow night."

Tory stifled her groan when she recognized that deep voice. She was too tired to spar with J.D.

She turned in a sleek, slow movement, tilting her chin so that she met his gaze straight on. "You're right, J.D.," she purred.

She knew the surprise wouldn't register anywhere other than his eyes, so that's where she kept her attention. She waited until the gray turned dark, almost smoky. "I'm working tomorrow night."

She brushed past him, holding crisp bills in her fist. The bartender tried to hide his laugh behind his hand. Tory felt triumphant as she placed the change in front of Grif.

"What d'ya say to him?" Grif asked, nodding in the direction of J.D.

"I told him no," she replied honestly.

"Good for you," Grif grumbled, peeling off some of the bills before pocketing the rest. "But he don't look too inclined to take no for an answer."

That wasn't her concern, she told herself as she lingered, clearing off the tables. She even checked Susan's tables, delaying her return to the bar until she could find no other alternative.

She noted J.D. quietly watched her from his seat near the jukebox, taking the occasional pull on a longneck bottle of beer. His scrutiny was wreaking havoc with her nerves. I'm just tired, she insisted to herself as she re-counted one stack of crumpled bills for the third time. She soon gave up and settled for an estimate of her earnings, then divided out the appropriate percentage for the bartender.

"Thanks," she called down to him, waving the bills and tucking them beneath an ashtray.

"Are you finished?" J.D. asked.

"Time to go home," she answered without looking at him.

"Not just yet."

"Not now, J.D.," she whined. "I'm too tired to play."

"I wasn't thinking of playing."

There was something disturbingly nonthreatening about his voice. Normally, nearly every syllable he flung at her held some sort of challenge. Grudgingly, she turned and met his hooded gaze. "What were you thinking of?"

He shrugged. "Call upstairs and let Rose know you're done for the night."

"Why?"

"She wants to talk to you."

"About what?"

"Tory." He said her name like an exasperated curse. "Just do it."

She did, though it annoyed her to do so.

He hadn't even bothered to make it sound like a request. It was an order. Nothing less. She wasn't too keen on orders, but Rose *was* her boss. She told herself she was responding to her ingrained respect for authority and not the infuriating finality of his instructions.

"You might want to get yourself a drink," J.D. suggested.

A chill ran along her spine just as the bartender and his conquest du jour sauntered out the door.

"Have you convinced your mother to fire me?" she asked, her head tilted, her eyes studying his immobile features. "That explains the tie. You've dressed for the occasion."

"I've dressed for the occasion, all right," he grumbled against the bottle he brought to his lips.

Tory watched his Adam's apple bob above the loosened collar of his shirt. He looked good in a white shirt and tie. It was a perfect contrast to his unkempt hair and the faint shadow of a beard he seemed to have no matter what the time of day. Recent days, working in the afternoon sun had turned his skin a deep shade of bronze. She thought it might also have hardened the muscles that sculpted every inch of his solid body.

"I think I'll get that drink now," she said, hoping it might douse the heat churning in the pit of her stomach. Grabbing a glass, she poured a healthy amount of wine and fortified herself with a quick sip before joining him at the table.

He leaned back in his chair with that casual arrogance that both annoyed and intrigued her. Tory wondered when she had developed these self-abusive tendencies. It wasn't her style to be interested in a man like J.D. Quite the contrary, she avoided his type like the plague.

"I can almost hear your mind working," he said finally.

"I'm impressed," she returned, drowning the butterflies in her stomach with a swallow of wine. "I didn't think you'd noticed I had a mind."

She wanted to reach out and grab the words and shove them back down her throat. Unfortunately, that wasn't an option.

J.D. leaned forward, elbow on the table. His eyes held hers briefly before he meaningfully allowed his gaze to drop lower, to where her body strained against the flimsy fabric of her uniform. "I've noticed everything about you, Tory. Your mind—" he paused and drank "—and your other attributes." His voice was liquid with promise, his eyes flickered with just a hint of the desire she heard in his words.

Shoving her chair back, she was torn between tossing the rest of her drink in his face and jumping into his lap.

"Sorry it took me so long," Rose said as she came upon them.

Tory was half out of her seat—and completely out of her mind.

Rose stood next to the table, her eyes moving between Tory and her stoic companion. As usual, Rose's appearance acted like a shut-off valve where J.D. was concerned. His expression closed and locked. He appeared so cool, aloof and distant, Tory wondered if she might have imagined the scene between them. This robot couldn't possibly be capable of any human emotion, certainly not lust or desire. Not with the flat look he donned every time his mother entered the room.

"I've found a solution to your problem," Rose began.

"Sorry," Tory said with an exaggerated sigh. "I think you're about thirty-five years too late to be putting him up for adoption," she whispered for J.D.'s benefit alone.

Direct hit, she thought as she watched his eyes narrow for just an instant.

"Victoria!" Rose said with a snort as she fell into the chair between them. "I was talking about your problems at school."

That got her attention. Tearing her eyes away from him, she urged a smile to her lips. "I'm sorry, Rose. You were saying?"

Rose produced the battered paperback directory of college funding and slipped her perfectly manicured, bloodred nail to a place marked by a plastic stirstick.

"I've been all through this, and I found a grant that will cover your tuition."

Tory regarded the woman speculatively. She'd been through it too and had found nothing.

"Right here," Rose announced, her lips pursed as she tapped the entry. "This is perfect."

Tory slid the book closer and read the entry. The Charleston Ladies Foundation provided up to twenty thousand dollars to an applicant enrolled in graduate studies in an accredited college or university. The funds were available only to women who were residents of South Carolina; there was no age limit set; and there was no differential for private versus state colleges.

"It's fine," Tory said, trying to keep her frustration in check. "But I'm not eligible," she explained. "Read the last requirement."

"I know," Rose said excitedly, rubbing her hands in front of her face. "This is simply too perfect."

Tory wondered for a brief moment if Rose had been spending too much time with Susan. Her normally down-to-earth boss was almost as out of touch with reality as her spaced-out employee. "I don't qualify," Tory repeated, saying each word slowly. "I'm not married. The grant is for married women only."

"That's where I come in," J.D. spoke up. "I'm going to marry you."

Chapter Five

"This is crazy." Tory managed to strangle the words from her tight, dry throat. "Marry you?"

"It's the perfect solution," Rose insisted.

Tory gaped at her boss. Didn't she see that the suggestion was neither perfect nor a solution?

"What's wrong, Tory?" J.D. asked in a slow, careful tone, as if they were discussing something as benign as the weather. "You said you were willing to do *anything* to finish your degree."

"Anything *sane*," she retorted. "And legal. Pretending to be married to you would amount to committing fraud."

"But we won't be pretending," he countered easily.

Wide-eyed, she regarded him for a long moment. She suddenly found his cool control infuriating. Nothing of what he was thinking was evident from the relaxed way his large body lounged back in the chair. Anger, tinged with just a hint of curiosity, simmered in the pit of her stomach as she took in the bland expression on his handsome face.

"If you're of a mind to help me, why don't you just lend me the money?"

"No collateral," J.D. answered with a sigh.

"I'd be happy to sign a note."

"Which," he said, speaking now in a louder, more even voice, "wouldn't be worth the paper it was written on."

"But after I get my degree—"

"There's no guarantee you'll find employment."

Digging her nails into her palms, Tory wanted to slap that superior smirk off his face. She had the sinking suspicion that she was being manipulated by a master. She just couldn't figure out why.

"Rose?" J.D.'s eyes never left Tory's face as he addressed his mother. "Would you mind leaving us alone to finish this discussion?"

Tory wasn't too thrilled with the idea of being left alone with J.D., not when he was in one of his steamroller moods. But voicing her fears would only give him another weapon for his already full arsenal.

"This can work," Rose insisted as she gave Tory's hand a squeeze. Leaning over, Rose added in a whisper, "Don't cut your nose off to spite your face. Pride's a cold bedfellow when it costs you your dreams."

Rose's footsteps echoed and died into an uncomfortable silence. Tory's heart was pounding against her ribs. She wondered why she didn't just thank him politely and walk out the door.

"You're about to tell me to take my proposal and stick it in my ear, aren't you?"

Tory felt her cheeks color. "Basically."

"You won't, though. Your education means too much to you."

"Not enough to commit fraud."

"I told you," he explained with exaggerated patience, "it won't be fraud. The marriage will be legal—and real."

"Define real." Tory chewed on her bottom lip.

J.D.'s eyes gleamed. "I think I'll leave that up to you."

"How uncharacteristically chivalrous of you," she said. Then she watched his eyes darken to a threatening, shimmering silver.

"If you want me to set the boundaries of our marriage, I would be more than willing."

Her stomach clenched as she digested the subtle meaning of his words. "That won't be necessary. We can't possibly get married."

"Why not?"

A short breath of exasperation spilled from her opened mouth. "Because we can't!"

"Why?" he asked quietly.

His calm had her teetering left of center. Trying to regain some semblance of rationality, Tory nervously twisted the hairs at the nape of her neck with trembling fingers. "Because it isn't right."

"Right for whom?"

"For you. Or me, either."

"I'm willing," he assured her with an easy half smile. "So that leaves you."

Her head tilted to one side. "Why are you so willing?"

The half smile widened into a wolfish grin. "The usual reasons."

His words caressed her as her mind brought forth heated images of his large hands on her body. Grasping her wineglass by the stem, she brought it to her lips and averted her eyes. "I'm sure you can find a willing partner without getting married, J.D."

"No doubt," he agreed without any real conceit.

"Then why?"

"Because Rose asked me to."

Peering over the rim of her glass, Tory found his gray eyes unusually cold. "So you're doing this to please your mother?"

"Among other things."

Her chin came up proudly. "If you've finally decided to be nice to your mother, why not start with something simple? Like treating her to dinner? Or coloring a picture she can hang on the refrigerator?"

The chuckle was little more than a rumble deep in his throat. "So what's it going to be, Victoria?"

The sound of her name on his lips stilled her breath. "I've already told you, this whole idea is preposterous."

"It is a bit...unconventional."

"Nose rings are unconventional," she said. "Marrying a man I don't know, or particularly li—"

"Like?" he interrupted. One eyebrow arched in a high taunt.

Tory sighed. "We don't exactly get along like best buddies."

"No," he agreed. "But I think you can learn to be nice to me, given time."

She was incensed. The adolescent urge to throw something at his sneering face was almost overwhelming. "*Nice?* You think I need to learn to be *nice* to you? That seals it," she said through clenched teeth as she rose from her chair. "Thanks, but no thanks, J.D. I'll find some other, *reasonable* way to finish school."

His hand shot out and caught her wrist. It was a steely hold, yet it didn't hurt. J.D., as usual, was in full control of his power. She knew that, even before she looked up to briefly meet his stormy gaze.

He loomed above her, his breath washing over her face. The scent of soap and cologne hung in the scant space between her body and his. His other hand hung at his side, his thumb brushing the pads of his fingertips. Tory concentrated on the pattern of his tie.

"Look at me."

It was an order, and she was not about to submit to his command. She didn't move so much as an eyelash.

The hand on her wrist moved, slowly working its way up her arm, leaving her skin feeling warm and alive on its path. His fingers glided over her shoulder until he found the underside of her chin. Gently, but with authority, J.D. nudged with enough pressure to force her to meet his eyes.

His thumb worked its way up over her chin, coming to rest just beneath her lower lip. His eyes fixed on her lips and then narrowed as his thumb gently explored the contours of her mouth.

Pressing her lips together, Tory fought a sudden burst of desire-inspired curiosity.

J.D. smiled, apparently all too happy to meet the challenge of her tight-lipped response. She expected his hard mouth to come crashing down on hers. But it didn't happen that way. J.D.'s free hand snaked around her waist, though he didn't pull her against him. His fingers simply rested against her hip. The hand on her mouth moved slowly, deliberately. She was keenly aware of the heat of her skin where his palm rested against her cheek. His thumb continued a slow, thorough assault on her lower lip. Her breath stilled as he gradually increased the pressure as well as the scope of exploration. He ran his thumb roughly across her mouth until her lips parted of their own volition. It was strange and exhilarating to watch the intense expression on his face as he followed the movements of his thumb. The pressure increased, until her lower lip was malleable and hot beneath his expert touch. It was a heady experience—more exciting than any kiss.

"Marry me," he said quietly, drawing his hand away from her face.

"I can't."

"Yes, you can."

Squeezing her eyes shut for a second, Tory composed herself. Did this jerk actually think his touch would render her stupid?

Tory stepped away from him and glared up at him. "I will not marry you. I am not that desperate."

"Yes, you are," he countered with a sigh as he leaned against the table.

"Earth to J.D. Did you think all you had to do was put your hands on me and I'd abandon all reason?"

He offered a roguish grin. "I wouldn't have minded."

"It won't happen. Just as this silly notion of our getting married won't happen."

"Yes, it will."

"God," she groaned. "What does it take to get through to you? I appreciate what you're trying to do, but I am not going to marry you."

His eyebrows drew together as he stood watching her, obviously lost in private thought. "How about if I sweeten the pot?"

"J.D.," she began reasonably, "you, yourself, acknowledged that school is the most important thing in the world to me. If I won't marry you to finish my education, what could you possibly offer me that could change my mind?"

His expression never faltered when he said, "Your mother."

"M-my mother?"

"As long as we're married, I'll see to it that your mother receives the best possible care."

Tory closed her eyes. The long list of expensive therapies scrolled through her mind. Things Dr. Trimble had said were too expensive and impractical to try, given her limited financial resources.

Opening her eyes slowly, willing all thought from her mind, she said simply, "Pick a date."

She'd expected to see a flash of triumph, something to symbolize his victory. She hadn't bargained on the relief she saw on his face. It was almost her undoing.

"I'll drive you home," he suggested.

"That isn't necessary."

"But it is," he assured her as he anchored her elbow in his hand. "We still have some details to hammer out."

TORY LEFT HIM in the small living room and sought refuge behind the safety of her bedroom door. "I should tell him to forget it," she mumbled as she stripped off her uniform. "I'm crazy for even considering this."

Tugging on a pair of faded, denim shorts, Tory pulled an oversize sweatshirt from her closet and slipped it over her head. Absently, she fluffed the top of her hair with her fingers as she searched for her sneakers. She gave up after a few minutes when she realized she was just delaying the inevitable. Straightening, she mustered all her courage and practiced a small speech in her mind.

Sorry, J.D., but I've thought it over and this is nuts. Have a nice night. She moaned audibly. Something told her J.D. wouldn't be so easily dismissed.

She found him lounging on the sofa, the knot of his loosened tie slightly askew in relation to his open collar. His eyes roamed over her entire body as she moved forward. His blatant appraisal did little to fortify her resolve.

"So," he began slowly, "have you decided on which way you're going to tell me to take a hike?"

Her eyes narrowed. She wasn't too thrilled to realize how easily this man could anticipate her thoughts.

"Yes, as a matter of fact, I've decided on a polite kiss-off," she told him with a saccharine smirk.

J.D. smiled then. She noted a small measure of something strangely reminiscent of regret in the action. "Sorry, doll. It's not going to be that easy."

"Something tells me nothing about you is easy."

"See?" he said, crossing one leg and grasping his ankle with both hands. "You're learning."

Tory gave him a stern, reproachful look. "And you're patronizing." She considered his half smile for a long time, then relented and offered one of her own.

"We'll get married at the end of the week," he said.

"So soon?" She hoped her voice revealed none of her shock at hearing his plan.

"That way, you can apply for the grant in plenty of time before the fall quarter starts."

"And you?" she asked. "Why are you *really* doing this, J.D.?"

Rubbing his hand across his chin, J.D.'s expression closed, the easy smile vanished. "I've already explained my reasons, Tory. Now I think we should get down to the nitty-gritty, so to speak."

Lacing her fingers together, Tory found herself interested, in spite of her vacillating thoughts about reneging on the deal. Listening to his proposal held the promise of a real experience, if nothing else.

"We won't tell anyone about our 'reasons' for getting married," he said.

"That might be tough," she countered. "They'll probably figure this isn't a match made in heaven when they realize we have separate addresses."

"But we won't have separate addresses."

"You can't think that I would even consider—"

"Sleeping with me?" he finished, struggling with a twinge of amusement at the corner of his mouth.

"I believe I've already told you where you stand on that issue, J.D."

"Yes." His smile broadened into a satisfied grin. "Well, the rules have changed."

"Not my rules."

"I'm making the rules now, Tory."

"Then I'm not going through with this farce," she told him flat out.

"Yes, you will. And you'll do it on my terms."

"Really?"

"Really. Marrying me will give you all the things you want."

"Such as?"

"School," he said evenly. "And I'll take care of your mother."

"I think I'll pass, just the same," Tory said with a smile.

"No, you won't," J.D. said with a dismissive little shake of his head. "You'll marry me because it's a viable solution to all your problems. You're a smart lady, you'll do the smart thing."

"You're very sure of yourself, aren't you, J.D.?"

"Yep," he said as he rose, stretching his long legs.

"This time you're going to be disappointed."

"Not by you, doll."

HIS CRYPTIC REMARK followed her into a fitful sleep. It was also the first thing she thought of when she woke the next morning. That disturbed her. Why was she having so much trouble putting J.D. and his ridiculous proposal into perspective? "Marry him," she scoffed as she pulled on her robe. "Not flaming likely."

Several sharp raps on her door summoned her from the task of filling the coffeepot. Gripping the edges of her robe, Tory opened the door a crack and peered out.

"Why are you here?" she said with a groan. "I thought we said everything we had to say last night."

"We did," J.D. answered. "Which is why I'm here."

"Haven't you ever heard it's rude to go visiting before 10:00 a.m.?"

"Doesn't apply," he said. He left her to glare at his back as he moved into the kitchen.

His broad shoulders were encased in a soft cotton pullover in a shade of muted gray that matched his eyes. His jeans were snug, hugging his tapered hips and well-defined thighs. His hair was still damp, and it curled slightly where it brushed the collar of his shirt.

"You're exempt from all the normal social graces?" she queried as she belted her robe.

"Nope," he answered as he opened the cabinet and took down a mug. "But I don't think we have to adhere to antiquated social traditions when we're engaged to be married."

Tory felt a mound of tension pool at the top of her spine. "We aren't getting married."

"Well," he said reasonably, leaning against the counter. "Not today."

"Good," Tory said with mock relief. "Because I have to be at work by eleven-thirty, so we'd be pressed for time."

"No you don't."

"No I don't what?" she asked, dreading his next words.

"You don't have to work today."

Sudden fury narrowed her eyes. "What have you done?"

His shrug pulled the fabric of his shirt taut against the vast expanse of muscle sculpting his broad chest. "I thought we should spend some time together before the wedding. Rose agreed."

"Well, I didn't," she said indignantly. "I need to work, J.D. I need the money, *damn it!*"

"I know that," he told her in that patronizing, low voice. "And I have no objection to your continuing to work after we're married. I just think we need to take a little time out to get to know each other before the end of the week."

"Stop it," she said, balling her fists at her sides as she tilted her head back to meet his bemused gray eyes.

"We are not getting married. I thought I made myself perfectly clear last night."

"You accepted my proposal last night."

"I took it back!" she wailed in frustration.

"Minor detail," he remarked. His thick, inky lashes fluttered above his eyes until his expression became strangely seductive.

His eyes wandered over her face, taking in each feature before roaming boldly down to the front of her robe. Her cheeks burned from his frank appraisal, but not, she discovered dejectedly, from embarrassment. If she closed her eyes, Tory knew she would remember the rough tenderness of his thumb on her mouth. A coil of desire tightened in her stomach.

Moving with the fluid ease that typified all his actions, J.D. pulled her against him, bracing his legs apart so that she was firmly wedged in the valley of his thighs. His hands dipped beneath her arms, his fingers locked behind the slope at the small of her back. Her palms flattened against his chest.

Her emotions were in chaos. The heat and power emanating from this man were a near-lethal combination. He made absolutely no move to kiss her, to touch her more intimately. He seemed content to simply have her in his arms. Her eyes fixed on his mouth, on the rigid set of his jaw. She could feel the even rise and fall of his chest beneath her fingers.

"Tory?"

Why did that single word have to sound so breathy? "Yes."

"There's an item in this morning's paper about your father. The police lab has confirmed it was murder."

"I knew that from the moment you discovered his body."

"It could have been suicide."

"No," she said as she carefully pushed out of his arms. "My father wouldn't have taken his own life."

"You're sure?"

Tory nodded and lowered her head, away from his intense inspection. "Very sure."

"The police will begin an investigation."

"I'm sure they will," she agreed. "But I wonder how much success they'll have, given the fact that almost fifteen years have passed."

"If you marry me, I can protect you."

"Protect me from what?" she asked.

"From whatever the police dig up."

Tory laughed nervously. "I hardly need to be protected, J.D. Nothing the police learn could possibly hurt me."

"Maybe," he returned. "But what about your mother? If you marry me, I won't ever tell them that you think she's the killer."

Chapter Six

An insistent series of sharp knocks split the silence, dividing J.D. and Tory.

"That's probably Detective Greer," he told her. "I want your answer."

It took all his concentration to keep his expression bland as he watched the play of emotion in her big blue eyes. He recognized and understood the defiance and confusion—along with a small speck of desire she tried so hard to conceal. He was not, however, pleased to see fear win out as she regarded him warily, arms crossed just beneath the rounded curved of her breasts.

He waited, trying not to be distracted by the hint of turquoise lace peeking at him from where the folds of her robe met.

The knock sounded again.

"I've got to get that," she hedged, but J.D. planted himself between her and the door.

"I want your answer now, Tory. Will you marry me?"

Her bowlike mouth pulled into a tight line, and her eyes flashed her fury as she flung her reply at him like a gauntlet. One he found himself quite content to accept.

"Yes."

"Then let's not keep the detective waiting."

Her disposition didn't improve with the arrival of yet another uninvited person. J.D. wondered how long it would be before huge puffs of dark smoke billowed from her ears. If her jerky movements and clipped speech were any indication, she was one angry lady.

After showing Detective Greer into her apartment, Tory regarded both men with blatant hostility. "J.D. can keep you company while I throw on something more appropriate," she said before marching off and closing the door to her bedroom with a wall-shattering slam.

J.D. smiled at the shorter man. "Morning isn't her best time."

Greer shrugged and seated himself on the sofa. J.D. knew Rose disliked this man because of something that had happened to the Tanners' son, Chad. But he was willing to reserve judgment. At least for the time being.

"So Bob Conway's death was definitely murder?"

The police detective regarded him briefly before giving a slight nod of his balding head. "So they tell me." Greer shifted, pulling a small notebook from the inside pocket of his jacket. Wetting one finger, he flipped through the first third of the pages, then he rummaged and finally produced a pen.

"You're Mrs. Porter's son."

It wasn't a question, so J.D. remained stoic as he took a seat across from the man.

"Joseph Porter?"

"I prefer J.D.," he corrected. "It saved me from that wonderful southern tradition of being called Junior or Little Joe."

"Smart move," Greer commiserated. "You visiting Charleston?"

"I'm here working. I'm going to do some renovations for Rose."

Greer's eyes raised inquisitively at his use of his mother's given name, but J.D. didn't feel the need to explain.

"Where do you live?"

"Miami area."

"But you came all the way up here to hammer a few nails."

J.D. turned at the feminine grunt of disgust Tory made as she rejoined them. She glanced at the chair next to J.D., but apparently opted to stand.

He didn't think much of her outfit, but then he didn't think much of her fashion sense in general. Today she had gone for a safari motif. Baggy shorts and a baggy shirt that hung loosely from her small shoulders. The clothes nearly swallowed her, but he also knew they accomplished her purpose.

"J.D. is an architect, Detective," she said in a slightly amused voice. Sorting through a stack of architectural magazines on the table, she pulled one free and flipped to the center feature. J.D. remembered that project well.

"This is just one example of his work."

Leaning back, he studied her profile, wondering if he should read anything into her knowledge of his professional accomplishments. Probably not, he decided. She'd already made it perfectly clear that she didn't much care for his modern buildings.

"Nice," Greer said.

J.D. brought his hand to his mouth to hide a snicker. The detective's single adjective would have been an insult to the investors who had paid a sizable price for the design and construction.

"Anyway—" Tory tossed the magazine on the floor and feathered her bangs nervously "—what did you want to see me about?"

"I just wanted to let you know what we're doing about your father's murder."

"That isn't necessary."

Her comment earned her the undivided attention of the law enforcement officer. "I should think you would be very interested in our investigation into the murder." The detective leveled his eyes on Tory and added, "He was shot once in the back of the head." He paused, apparently waiting for her reaction. Tory wasn't about to comply.

"Almost execution-style," he added.

Tory blandly asked, "Will your grisly little diatribe bring back my father?"

Excellent comeback, J.D. thought as he mentally placed a tally in her column. He'd bet a year's profit that Tory had no idea what a powerful weapon her honesty was. Too late, he asked himself how she might react to learning of his deception.

"Of course not," Greer answered in a clipped, official-sounding voice. "I just wanted to assure you that my department will investigate this matter fully."

"I'm sure you will," Tory told him without inflection.

"How old were you when your father disappeared?"

"Ten, almost eleven."

"And your mother was . . . ?"

"Still a functioning member of society."

J.D. heard none of the bitterness he might have expected. Only sadness and regret. He didn't like the swell of compassion building in his chest.

"Yes, well," Greer stammered. "Would you mind explaining her illness to me?"

"My mother had a nervous breakdown after my father disappeared. She isn't expected to recover."

"Do you mind if I interview her?"

J.D. intercepted the question. "I think that decision would be best handled by her physician."

"Just what is your interest in all this, Mr. Porter?" Greer asked.

"Tory is my fiancée. We're getting married at the end of the week."

Greer's brown eyes volleyed between him and the rigid woman standing next to him. J.D. reached for her hand and found it clammy.

"I see," Greer said with an unconvinced nod. "I was under the impression that you had just recently come to Charleston."

"What can I say?" J.D. said as he got to his feet. He tugged Tory against him, molding her soft body to his side. She wasn't exactly pliant, but she didn't jerk away, either. He figured it was a start.

"He can't say anything," he heard Tory tell the detective. "Words couldn't begin to describe what's happened between us in such a short time."

J.D. lowered his head until his mouth was next to her ear and his nostrils filled with the subtle floral fragrance of her hair. "Careful, doll," he whispered as he brushed his lips against her exposed earlobe. He smiled as he felt the small shudder in her body.

"I guess you could say J.D. and I have decided we simply can't live without each other," she said as she placed a tentative hand at his waist, apparently trying to add conviction to her statement.

If his expression was any indication, Greer was willing to accept it for the moment, but J.D. wasn't certain that the detective was buying into the love-at-first-sight routine.

Greer wet the end of his pencil with the tip of his serpentlike tongue and turned his focus back on Tory. "What can you tell me about the time your father disappeared?"

Her hand fell away from his waist and he could sense the sudden tension emanating from her small frame. "I was just a little girl back then. All I remember is that my father—whom I loved dearly—stopped coming home."

"What about before his disappearance? Did he seem distracted? Did he fight with anyone? Did he—"

Tory visibly shivered and moved over to the window. "He gave me rides on his back through the bar before it opened. We played hide-and-seek in the dependency. He let me squirt the soda water into the sink whenever my mother wasn't around. No matter how busy the bar was, he always came up at nine-thirty and kissed me good-night."

She spun on the ball of her bare foot, her resentful glare shooting daggers into Greer. "Those are the things I remember, Detective Greer. And I don't think any of those memories will help you find his killer."

Without skipping a beat, Greer asked, "And your mother?"

"Always smelled like the grease from the kitchen." Tory paused just long enough to take in a deep breath, then stared into space as she spoke. "Even though she waited tables until the wee hours of the morning, my mother always got up to make my breakfast. She checked my homework and kissed my boo-boos. In those days, she was always perfectly made-up, and her blond hair was usually in a long braid. She used to let me tie the ribbon at the end of it as a special reward." Rigidly, Tory turned back to the men.

Her eyes moved to Greer's notepad, where the detective hadn't written a word. J.D. felt as if someone had kicked him in the gut. Though her descriptions were vivid and emotional, her expression was completely blank.

"So," Tory continued, "I think you're wasting your time interrogating me. I was too young and too naive to remember anything significant. I was a sheltered, only child. Even if there was some sort of problem, neither of my parents would have breathed a word of it to me."

Greer nodded thoughtfully as he got to his feet. J.D. could see Tory relax as the detective prepared to leave.

She reached for the door and politely held it open for him. Greer stopped suddenly when he had one foot on the threshold. "The place was called the Rusty Nail when your family owned it, right?"

"Yes," she answered.

"Do you remember any of the employees?"

"I wasn't allowed downstairs once the bar opened," Tory told him, clearly becoming annoyed. "You seem to keep forgetting that I was a child at the time."

"So," Greer said as he peered at her over his shoulder, "you weren't aware of the fact that the current owner was a waitress when your folks owned the place?"

"Rose?" Tory said with a gasp.

"Six nights a week," Greer supplied with what seemed like rather perverse satisfaction.

Tory leaned against the door as if her legs had suddenly turned to mush. "She never said anything to me."

"I knew," J.D. said quietly.

Instantly he felt her intense blue eyes questioning him.

"Rose sent letters to us when we were kids. She mentioned where she worked."

"Us?" Greer asked.

"My younger brother, Dr. Wesley Porter."

"How can I reach him?" Greer demanded, quickly gathering the necessary materials from his rumpled jacket.

"He's in Miami now," J.D. answered. "But he'll be here at the end of the week for the wedding."

Tory's eyes grew wide as the detective pursed his thin lips and nodded. "I'll wait until he's here. But please let your brother know that I'll need to speak to him before he leaves Charleston."

"No problem," J.D. said.

Greer moved a fraction of an inch before turning to a stunned Tory one last time. "Does the name Evan Richards mean anything to you?"

"No," she answered quickly.

Too quickly, J.D. thought. And judging by Greer's slight hesitation, the detective had picked up on it, too.

"I'll be in touch," Greer promised.

When she closed the door, she leaned against it, looking tense and fully exhausted. J.D. allowed his eyes to linger on the hint of skin at the base of her throat near the top button of her shapeless shirt. Just the smallest insinuation of cleavage teased his senses— senses he was certain he had completely lost when he'd agreed to participate in this incredible scheme his mother had cooked up.

"Well?" she asked him on an impatient breath.

"Well what?"

"How did you know to get here one step ahead of Greer?"

"He called Rose," he said with a shrug. "She called me."

The frown marring her pretty mouth appeared to lessen as she digested his explanation. Of course, she had no way of knowing that Rose had told him much more than just the simple matter of Detective Greer's zealous interest in the fifteen-year-old murder.

"May I have something to drink?" he asked in a polite voice that his well-educated stepmother would have applauded.

"Coffee?"

He shook his head. "Something cold. It's mighty hot out there."

"Spoken like a true Floridian," she quipped as she moved into the kitchen.

Her movements were fluid, soft—and they exuded a certain naive femininity that belied her smart mouth and above-average intelligence. Sitting on the lumpy sofa, he listened to the sounds from the kitchen—ice being twisted from the tray, the protesting squeal of the aged refrigerator being opened. He also thought about Tory. She was going to be his wife.

The word alone should have brought perspiration to his forehead, a tremor to his hands and severe nausea to his midsection. Instead, he discovered that he was actually consumed with curiosity.

Okay, he thought as he adjusted himself away from an attack coil in the sofa cushion, the worst-case scenario is we play this charade out for a year. Long enough for Tory to get her degree.

"Hell," he mumbled under his breath, "a person can do anything for a year."

His mind suddenly flashed to an image of Tory and him, tangled in the sheets of his big bed, making mad, passionate love to each other. Now his body did react, though not in the obvious fashion. His palms became clammy, droplets of sweat began to form just above his upper lip and his chest was suddenly tight with a mixture of emotions he wasn't yet ready to acknowledge or define. Of course, if Tory knew the real reason for the marriage, she'd probably use the sheet to hang him from the ceiling.

CARRYING A STEAMING MUG of coffee in one hand and a tall glass of iced tea in the other, Tory had run out of things to delay her in the kitchen. For some unexplained reason, J.D. had the uncanny ability to make her nervous. Luckily, she didn't think it showed as she leaned forward to place his glass on the stack of magazines in front of him on the table.

She settled for a seat at the rickety table across from him, holding her mug in both hands as she brought it to her lips. She watched with complete fascination as his large, nimble fingers squeezed the wedge of lemon into the tea. How, she wondered, could such large hands be capable of such delicate movement? She swallowed without really tasting. J.D.'s appearance of total control made her as tense as it made her curious.

The lemon wedge was simply a metaphor for what bothered her most about this attractive man. Instead of gently and precisely squeezing the juice into the glass, he could just as easily have crushed it between his massive thumb and forefinger. Heat found its way to her cheeks when she envisioned what it might be like to have those fingers against her flesh.

"Hot?" J.D. queried.

"What?" she chirped, then "Damn it!" as she sloshed coffee on herself.

J.D. remained expressionless as he watched her futile attempt to blot the stain from the leg of her shorts. "I was just asking if you were warm. You looked flushed there for a minute."

Keeping her eyes downcast, Tory said, "I was just replaying the visit from the detective."

"They discovered a body. The police have to investigate."

"It was a skeleton," she corrected quickly, still unwilling to meet his gaze. "And it was fifteen years ago. I'm sure the Charleston Police Department has more pressing matters to attend to than waste their time on how my father died."

"Don't you mean *why?*"

Her head came up then, her eyes wide as they collided with his intense gray gaze. "Why?"

"The man was murdered. If it were my father, I'd want to know why."

"Well," she retorted hotly, squaring her shoulders, "he wasn't your father, so don't presume to tell me what I should be feeling."

"Is that really the reason?" he asked, his voice soft, soothing and irritatingly kind.

"Of course."

"Are you *that* certain your mother killed him?" J.D. asked after a brief silence.

Tory virtually ran into the kitchen, her heart pounding from the secret pain she'd been feeling ever since they'd discovered her father's remains. Bracing her palms against the damp edge of the sink, she sucked in deep breaths of the odd mixture of freshly cut lemon and coffee grounds.

A new scent was added a few minutes later. A purely masculine scent that told her J.D. had joined her in the kitchen area. The fact that his presence was comforting on some level was almost as strange as the fact that she had agreed to marry this virtual stranger. *Marry.* The word made her swallow the thick lump lodged in her throat.

Soundlessly, he moved behind her until she could feel the hard outline of his body against her back. The feel of him only managed to further scramble her already jumbled thoughts.

"What if you're wrong?"

"I've been telling you that all along," she answered. "While I appreciate the offer, something tells me marrying you will be a colossal mistake."

She felt him stiffen.

"I was referring to your belief that your mother is the killer."

It was her turn to tense. "Gee, J.D., maybe we can run on out to Ashley Villas and ask her. Or better yet," she continued, her voice sharp and slightly angry as it thundered through the small room, "maybe she'll confess to Detective Greer and save us all from endless speculation."

His hands clamped on her shoulders, his grasp tempered as he spun her to face him. "I was only suggesting that maybe you're wrong about your mother."

Tory's whole body felt heavy whenever she thought of her mother's present state. "Do you have any idea how long I've wondered why my mother fell apart after my father disappeared?" she asked with genuine feeling. "Even though I was only a child, I knew instinctively that her breakdown was a reaction to her husband's having up and vanished."

"People react to things differently, Tory," he said as his fingers began a slow massage of her shoulders.

"You sound like my grandmother. She simply chalked up my mother's breakdown to her inherently weak character."

"And you didn't buy that?" he asked, one dark eyebrow arched upward.

"My mother wasn't a weak woman," she explained, feeling herself relax under his touch. "She was a tad on the subservient side when it came to my father, but she didn't get the vapors or anything."

His lopsided grin coaxed a small half smile from Tory.

"She lived to please my father and to care for me. She did everything but iron his underwear. The upstairs of the bar was as neat as a pin, and I always looked like the poster child for the Perfect Parenting Society."

"Then why did you lie to Greer?"

His accusation caused her to suck in a breath.

J.D. brushed his hand up over her throat until his warm, slightly callused palm rested against her cheek. "Maybe you didn't lie, but I had the distinct impression that you omitted some things about your recollections."

Shrugging away from him, Tory tried—futilely—to withdraw from him. Since she couldn't accomplish that, she settled for fixing her gaze on the front of his shirt.

"I don't know what you're talking about."

"Yes, you do."

"I was a child!" she wailed.

"A bright child who knew more than she just told the police."

Expelling her breath slowly, Tory met his eyes. "What do you expect me to do, J.D.? Tell the police that I think my own mother is a murderer?"

His expression softened. "I expect you to keep an open mind."

"Meaning?"

"Apparently, a lot was happening fifteen years ago."

Her head tilted off to one side and she regarded him for a short time. "What would you know about it? You weren't even here fifteen years ago."

"I wasn't," he admitted. "But Rose was."

"Excuse me?" Tory felt her eyes widen as she gaped at him.

"Rose worked for your parents. She did the nine-to-two shift, which is why you probably don't remember her. And she wasn't a child when all this was happening."

"Why hasn't she ever...?" Tory's voice trailed off as her brain assimilated this information.

"You were already working there when she and Shelby bought the place from Brewster. She said that when she found out what had happened to your mother, she was reluctant to bring it up."

"So why are you telling me this."

"Because it's the right thing to do."

"And why is that?"

"Because she has some theories of her own about the murder. And they don't match yours."

Chapter Seven

For the first time since the gruesome discovery of the skeleton, Tory felt a glimmer of hope. "Rose knows who murdered my father?"

"Not exactly," J.D. answered.

Exasperation oozed from every one of her pores as she stared up at the large man. As if sensing her growing frustration with him, J.D. grasped her hand and led her into the living room area.

He sat down, tugging her along with him so that she felt the coarseness of his jeans brush the side of her upper thigh through her shorts.

His eyes scanned her face, then he said, "Rose and Shelby will be here soon."

"For what?" she demanded.

His grin was boyishly shy, bordering on apologetic. "They've kind of appointed themselves your personal shoppers for the wedding on Friday afternoon."

Wedding ... Friday ... Good Lord, what had she gotten herself into?

"And while we're wasting the morning shopping, is your mother going to tell me who she thinks killed my father?"

She watched his expression. It closed and became as benign as a pair of blinds suddenly snapped shut.

"That's up to her," J.D. hedged. "I don't know how she'll want to handle all this."

"What is *all this?*" Tory practically screamed at him.

The annoying feel of his body pressed against the side of hers wasn't helping matters much. That little voice of reason told her she was simply too aware of this man. She'd been attracted to men before, but never with the intensity she felt whenever J.D. was within five miles of her. And it didn't make any sense. He personified everything she disliked in a man. *So why am I going to marry him in a matter of days?* she asked herself with amazement.

"Look," he began patiently. "Rose didn't tell me all that much, and what she did say, she said in confidence." His gray eyes darkened slightly before he added, "And I always keep confidences."

Tory frowned but knew full well that no amount of coaxing or pleading would get him to open up. Not J.D., the King of Control. Sighing loudly, she looked down at the coffee stain on her shorts, then she glanced at the cheap but reliable goldstone watch on her wrist. "Why are your mother and Shelby taking me shopping?"

J.D. rose and began the slow pace of a newly captured animal getting a feel for its cage. "Rose has insisted on a real ceremony."

"What?" Tory yelped.

J.D. didn't look at her, nor did he stop the fluid back-and-forth movements. "She's making arrangements to close the Rose Tattoo on Friday. She's already found a preacher and decided on flowers and—''

''Who the hell told her she could do all this?''

J.D. stopped abruptly and met her shocked gaze straight on. ''I did.''

This was getting out of hand, Tory thought. ''You mean to tell me that we're going through this sham of a marriage with all the frills and trimmings of the real thing? And no one bothered to so much as ask me if it was okay with me?''

''If we do it this way, we'll have pictures and witnesses to show the Charleston Ladies Foundation, should they wish to question the validity of our hasty marriage.''

''A certificate from a justice of the peace would surely be sufficient,'' Tory argued.

Bracing his feet a shoulder-width apart, J.D. looped his thumbs into the waistband of his jeans, his eyes boring into hers. ''Apparently, it is also very important to Rose that we do it this way. I know she and Shelby have helped you out in the past. Will it kill you to do this for her?''

Tory felt her cheeks burn with color. Rose and Shelby *had* been awfully good to her. Lacing her fingers together, she placed them in her lap and said, ''Of course it won't kill me. I just wish one of you would have discussed this idea with me before you set the wheels in motion.''

''I never touched the wheel,'' he returned, a certain edge to his voice. ''I'm pretty sure Rose has an ulterior motive for doing this.''

''Such as?''

''Wesley is flying up on Thursday night to act as best man.''

"Your brother?"

"So Rose gets her wish," J.D. began. "Both her sons in the same room at the same time."

Tory knew from years of hearing stories just how much the separation of her family hurt Rose. After a slight hesitation, she said, "Then I'll cooperate."

J.D.'s dark head tilted slightly to one side, conveying a mixture of surprise and gratification. "Can I expect you to give in to everything so easily once we're married?" he asked teasingly, a smile tugging at the corners of his mouth.

Tory grunted before telling him in no uncertain terms, "I'm agreeing to the ceremony for Rose. And we're going to be married in name only, so you needn't concern yourself with how or why I make my decisions."

With eyes as silver as a storm cloud, J.D. simply stared at her, his mouth a hard line.

Tory felt her palms grow damp in the nerve-racking silence that stretched between them. "What I meant to say was that since this isn't like a real marriage—"

"I'm renting a real tux. I'm paying a real photographer."

"J.D.," Tory said with a groan, rising from the sofa but remaining on the safe side of the scratched and scarred coffee table. "I'm trying to discuss the logistics of what will happen *after* this elaborate ceremony *I* just found out about."

"Logistics?" he repeated with a huge grin.

Rolling her eyes, Tory said a silent prayer for patience. "You're intentionally being obtuse."

"Are we talking about your conjugal responsibilities following the ceremony?"

"I won't have any conjugal responsibilities," she told him disdainfully.

J.D.'s grin graduated into a smile that produced phenomenally sexy dimples on either side of his mouth. "We'll see," he told her in an inviting tone.

Tory was about to launch into the many reasons that she would never agree to having any sort of sexual relationship with him, when he raised his hand in anticipation of her response.

"I'm supposed to tell you to be prepared to try on every wedding gown in Charleston." Just a hint of redness appeared against his cheeks. "But I think Rose already has a dress in mind for you."

"Really?" Tory asked cautiously. She could just imagine herself in a replica of the dress Priscilla Presley wore when she married Elvis. Knowing Rose, the consummate Elvis fan, Tory would probably be expected to wear a black wig and inch-long false eyelashes, to boot.

"Have fun," J.D. told her, adding a playful wink. "I'll be meeting you at the Tattoo when you're finished with Rose and Shelby."

"What for?"

"Lunch."

"Lunch?"

"The midday meal. Surely an educated woman like you knows what lunch is."

"I know what it is. I just don't know why we're having it together."

His bronze-colored fingers grasped the worn knob of the door, and he looked back at her over his broad shoulder. "It's usually called a date, Tory. I thought it might be nice for us to have at least one before the wedding."

With that, he was gone, leaving his words behind to taunt her as she went into the small bedroom to change her clothes.

ROSE ARRIVED with Shelby waddling a short distance behind, her balance hindered by the swell of her forthcoming child. Tory smiled at them both, even though what she really felt like doing was demanding an immediate halt to the whole ceremonial charade.

Rose's snug, leopard-print slacks outlined her generous hips, and a bright orange patent-leather belt cinched her small waist. A matching orange tank top and ten pounds of costume jewelry completed the look. It was a typical Rose ensemble, which Tory normally accepted without much notice. Today, she realized, was to be different—drastically so.

Rose stood in the center of the room, her hands clamped on her hips as she gave Tory a very unflattering once-over. "That gunnysack of a dress will be a pain in the rear every time you have to try on a gown."

"She has a point," Shelby chimed in as she lowered her swollen body into the closest chair. "I think I tried on three dozen dresses before I found my wedding gown."

Tory looked to the attractive, raven-haired woman and asked, "If you wouldn't mind letting me borrow yours, we can forget this whole shopping thing." Ignoring Rose's snort of protest, Tory continued, "You're in no condition to be traipsing all over Charleston in this heat looking for a dress for me."

"I'm not going," Shelby answered. "You and Rose are going to drop me off at the Tattoo on your way." Shelby ran her fingertips over her belly in what appeared to be soothing, circular motions. "And besides," Shelby added with a small smirk, "my dress would only fit you from the waist down. The Good Lord wasn't quite as generous with me when he handed out the breast DNA."

Tory felt herself blush furiously. While Shelby had a lovely figure when she wasn't pregnant, she wasn't anywhere nearly as top-heavy as Tory.

In one respect, Tory was glad she would have an opportunity to spend some time alone with Rose to discuss the murder of her father. On the other hand, it also meant she would be at the mercy of Rose's rather flamboyant, almost garish taste. It reminded her of a Christmas when she was about six. Santa had brought her the toy she'd been begging for for months, only he forgot the batteries. Shopping for a wedding dress alone with Rose was definitely going to be a forgotten-battery experience.

Rose pointed one long fingernail coated in bright orange polish in the direction of the bedroom and said, "Make sure you have on hose and something that doesn't have to be pulled over your head."

Tory moved on command.

"And don't dally. Dylan and J.D. will kill me if we don't get back to the Tattoo before the lunch crunch," Rose called after her.

Tory ran through the scant offerings in her closet with about as much enthusiasm as a person dressing for a trip to the dentist. "Wedding gown," she grumbled as she yanked a formless, floral-print dress from the closet. "If Rose wants buttons, she'll sure get 'em with this baby."

The dress buttoned at the throat, then at inch-and-a-quarter intervals it buttoned again, all the way down to where it brushed her ankles. The material swirled around her legs as she quickly made up the bed and slipped two gold-plate bracelets onto her wrist.

"Come on, Tory!" she heard Rose call out impatiently.

"Almost done," she called back, struggling to ease the last gold hoop into her ear.

Whatever her expectations when she joined her bosses, it wasn't the frown from Rose and the poorly hidden wince from Shelby. Tory felt instantly hurt and self-conscious. "I can change again," she told them.

"That isn't necessary," Shelby insisted as she got to her feet. The smile she offered was as warm and generous as the woman herself. "But..." Shelby hesitated. "You're going shopping for a wedding gown," she said in a voice softened by kindness. "That shapeless thing you're wearing will make it really hard for the sales people."

"Am I supposed to wear tights and a leotard?" Tory grumbled.

"That wasn't what Shelby was trying to say," Rose insisted. "I know you have this thing about hiding your body, but Friday *is* your wedding day." Rose gave a wicked wink and added, "You don't want J.D. to think he's marrying a sack of potatoes, do you?"

Had Shelby not been in the room, Tory would have told her future mother-in-law exactly what J.D. was marrying—a woman using a desperate measure to finish graduate school. Instead, her head held high, Tory turned on her heels, and headed back into her room.

"Something easy to take on and off," she mimicked as she scraped hangers across the rod. "Something that will show my shape so the salesperson won't have to waste her precious time guessing which dress might be appropriate for me.''

She finally settled on a beige blouse and tucked it into a short brown skirt. It took two safety pins to keep the front of the blouse from puckering at the closure near her overly ample breasts. Tory felt uncomfortable, but she was certain Rose would approve.

She was right.

"Good heavens, child!" Rose exclaimed as Tory returned to the living room. "If I had a body like that, I sure as hell wouldn't hide it the way you do."

Tory blushed profusely and crossed her arms in front of her chest.

"Just goes to show," Rose said philosophically as the trio left the dingy apartment, "we definitely aren't all created equal. Do you have any idea how much I pay for those fancy bras that create the illusion of cleavage?"

"I wouldn't have the faintest idea," Tory mumbled. "Could we please talk about something else?" she added, hugging her purse in front of her as she waited to take her seat in Rose's pink Cadillac.

The Elvis Presley air freshener swayed in time with the Elvis tune crooning softly from the cassette deck. Three songs later, Rose dropped Shelby off at the back entrance to the Tattoo.

"I see J.D. has already started the excavation on the dependency," Tory noted as she surveyed the mounds of freshly turned dirt and stone surrounding the building.

"That moron Greer wasn't too thrilled, but J.D. told him he had to get started since he's only staying in Charleston long enough to renovate the building. Of course he wasn't too thrilled that some bozo on his crew started digging before he got here, either."

An odd wave of sadness engulfed her at the thought of J.D. leaving Charleston. Tory shook her head, banishing the foolish thoughts from her brain. *I don't even like him, she reminded herself. I'm only marrying him for practical reasons.*

Rose barreled backward out of the alleyway as if they were being chased by the devil himself. Bracing herself against the dashboard, Tory tried to think of an appropriate way to broach the subject of her father's murder.

"We're going to Faye's," Rose announced as she cut off another driver in order to make a quick left into a parking lot less than three blocks from the Rose Tattoo. "Faye and I go way back. She'll take good care of us."

"Rose," Tory began softly, placing her hand on the other woman's forearm, "you're acting like a real mother of the groom."

Rose's professionally waxed eyebrows rose high on her forehead as she turned her eyes on Tory. Her expression still held that little thrilled look over the upcoming festivities, yet there was a tempering of reality there, as well.

"I know this marriage isn't exactly traditional, but that doesn't mean we have to treat it like a wake." Cutting the engine, Rose continued. "Wesley is coming in on Thursday to be fitted for his tux as best man. Hell," she said as she patted her stiff hair, "even my useless ex and the coed are flying up for the nuptials."

"What?" Tory squealed.

"J.D. was insistent that we treat this like a true love-at-first-sight thing."

"A best man? His father and stepmother?"

"It'll be a kick, don't you think?" Rose gleamed, a purely venomous look in her eyes. "I haven't seen the coed for years." Rose ran her hands along the slender outline of her waist and hips. "I hope she's gained a hundred pounds and lost all her teeth."

Tory regarded her companion for a second. "Are you still in love with J.D.'s father?"

"Hell, no," Rose grunted with a dismissive flick of her bejeweled wrist. "I'm just looking very forward to showing that weasel that I've made a good life for myself in spite of the fact that he walked out on me without so much as a glance backward."

Tory smiled, seeing the sparkle of anticipation in the other woman's expression. It suddenly dawned on her why this farce of a wedding was so important to her flamboyant employer. Tory's only reservation was keeping the reasons for the marriage a secret. She could still see Shelby's excited expression. And J.D.'s adamant proclamation that they tell no one of the circumstances behind the speedy wedding reverberated in her mind as they made their way into the shop.

It was a long, narrow building, with rows of frilly white and ivory dresses hanging on one side. On the opposite side she saw an eclectic collection of dresses meant for attendants and other members of the wedding party. To her utter relief, Tory saw nothing flashy or vulgar hanging on the racks.

A tall woman she guessed to be about Rose's age, and whom she assumed was Rose's friend Faye, appeared from behind a blue curtain at the rear of the shop. Unlike Rose, she wore a tailored ecru suit and tasteful jewelry. She flashed Rose a smile of instant recognition. Faye and Rose exchanged hugs, their perfumes competing in the process.

Faye turned and offered Tory her hand. "You must be the bride."

Tory only nodded, fighting the urge to yell, "No! I'm the fraud!"

"Do you have the dress?" Rose asked.

Faye nodded then turned her trained eye on Tory. "I'd guess a size six, but we'll probably have to alter an eight in order to accommodate her bosom."

Again with the boobs, Tory groaned inwardly.

"Follow me," Faye instructed. "Rose, help yourself to some tea. There's a table over there complete with lemon and sugar."

Dutifully, Tory followed Faye behind the blue curtain. It was like no other dressing room she'd ever been in. It was oval, with mirrored walls and a platform in the center. Off to the left she spotted several dresses encased in zippered, protective plastic.

"We'll try the six, but I don't think it will work."

Tory was directed into a small stall, with Faye toting the heavy dress. With utmost care, Faye unzipped the plastic and freed the gown from the covering. Tory's breath caught in her throat. Stunning didn't even begin to describe the delicate damask gown. Its off-the-shoulder neckline was trimmed with a tiny row of pearls, the pattern repeated along the edges, which would fall in the vicinity of her upper arms. It even had a train. A train long enough to be elegant without being ostentatious.

"Rose picked this dress?" she gasped.

Faye smiled. "She said your mother wore a similar gown when she married your father. Apparently, you showed her a picture or something." Faye suddenly looked stricken. "How indelicate of me to mention your father in light of recent events."

"No apology necessary."

Tory reached into her handbag and produced a faded black-and-white picture of her parents on their wedding day. While the gown wasn't exactly the same, it was quite close. She handed the photograph to Faye.

"Same style, the fabric doesn't match, but that's only a minor detail," Faye said, her smile growing into a definite leer. "And with your looks, J.D. will probably be oblivious to the difference."

"J.D.?"

Faye's naturally white eyebrows drew together questioningly. "When he left the deposit, he said you were to select whatever you wanted."

"J.D. was here?"

"Yesterday. He and Rose came by to see if I had anything in stock close to your mother's gown. With the wedding just days away, I wouldn't have time for a special order and alterations."

"And J.D. is footing the bill?"

Faye's smile bordered on condescension. "He mentioned that you were rather short on cash at the moment."

"That's an interesting way of putting it," Tory said under her breath.

Faye patted Tory's shoulder. "These days, it isn't at all uncommon for the bride and groom to pay their own expenses."

Tory immediately reached for the price tag and nearly choked when she saw the figure printed in neat dark letters.

Faye ripped the tag from her hand and made a tsking sound with her tongue. "J.D. left strict instructions that you were not to concern yourself with the price."

"That's my J.D.," Tory agreed with a snide smirk.

When Faye left her to try on the garment, Tory found herself considering referring to herself as Mrs. Autocratic after the wedding. J.D.'s propensity for issuing orders grated.

The dress fit perfectly, if she was willing to overlook the fact that the back could not be zipped up.

"How are we doing?" Faye called.

Tory stepped from the changing area and found Rose with Faye. Both women stared in appreciative awe as she stepped up onto the platform, damask swirling around her feet.

Tory's first vision of herself as a bride brought her to the verge of tears. Like most girls, she'd dreamed of this day. In her dreams, her father escorted her down the aisle. Her mother cried and dabbed at her eyes with one of those linen handkerchiefs she used to carry no matter what the occasion.

"We're going to have to go with the eight," Faye said, coming up behind Tory and tugging at the open edges of the bodice.

"Maybe we should try a different style," Tory suggested. The excessive amount of cleavage revealed by the dress was sexy, but she wasn't marrying J.D. for sex.

"Don't be silly," Rose said. "A daughter should follow in the tradition of her mother on her wedding day."

"But—"

"But nothing," Rose interrupted. "You've shown me that picture of your parents at least a hundred times. You're going to marry my son in a dress like the one your mother wore."

"But—"

"Rose is right," Faye said, sighing. "Years from now, you'll look back at your wedding pictures and be glad you held the tradition."

"Years from now—"

"You can't see into the future," Rose interrupted again. "Try on the eight."

Tory, disregarding her reservations, changed into the larger size. In less than a second, a woman with glowing brown skin appeared to pin the dress into a proper fit. The final result was nothing short of picture perfect, especially when Faye produced a silk bouquet for Tory to hold.

"Not up there," Rose moaned, reaching up to lower the flowers so that Tory was no longer able to discreetly cover her chest. "You hold it waist-high," she explained.

"It's a beautiful gown," Tory began, "but I feel so...exposed."

"Count your blessings." Faye chuckled. "Many of the young women who come in here want that particular cut but don't have the shape to carry it off."

"We'll take it," Rose announced. "Susan will be in tomorrow to be fitted for her dress."

"Susan?"

"I simply assumed that you would want her to serve as your maid of honor," Rose said. "If you'd prefer someone else..."

"No," she answered. "Susan is the perfect choice." Since her fellow waitress wasn't exactly the sharpest knife in the drawer, Tory figured the woman wouldn't catch on that the whole thing was a farce.

Tory nodded her way through the selection of flowers and an outfit for Rose. Then, with Faye's guidance, they made arrangements for a final fitting after the alterations and arranged a time for the gown to be picked up prior to the wedding.

"Take these out and start the car for me, would you?" Rose asked, handing Tory an Elvis key ring.

Tory used the ensuing five minutes to try to formulate a discreet way to broach the subject of her father with Rose. By the time Rose slid behind the wheel, Tory was ready.

"I hope all this wasn't too taxing for you," Rose commented. "I know you're just getting over the shock of them finding your daddy, and all."

This is too easy, Tory thought. "Of course I'm sorry to learn of his death, but somehow, and I know this sounds weird, it's easier knowing he's been dead all these years than trying to understand why he abandoned me and my mother."

In her peripheral vision, Tory watched Rose's expression grow hard, almost hateful.

"I'm sorry," she amended quickly. "I forgot about you and J.D.'s father."

"It isn't that," Rose responded quickly.

"J.D. told me that you had a theory about who might have killed my father."

Now Rose's expression did turn hateful. "Apparently, the coed didn't teach my boy when to keep his mouth shut."

Tory shifted and tucked one foot beneath her on the seat. She also reached over and lowered the volume on the perpetually playing Elvis tape. "If you know something, I think you should tell Detective Greer."

Rose grunted with total disgust. "That man couldn't solve a murder if it happened right in front of his beady little eyes."

Tory felt her stomach knot and tried to convince herself her queasiness resulted from the combination of the Elvis air freshener and Rose's perfume. Lacing her fingers in an attempt to keep her hands from shaking, it took Tory a long time to coax the question from her lips. "Do you think my mother shot my father?"

Rose's fingers froze on the steering wheel. Her head spun around quickly so that Tory could see her wide-open green eyes. "Your mama?" she repeated incredulously.

"I don't remember much," Tory admitted, "but I know they used to argue a lot."

"Gloria."

"Excuse me?" Tory asked.

"One of the other waitresses back when the Rose Tattoo was the Rusty Nail."

"You think she killed my father?"

"Who knows," Rose answered in a much softer tone. "I'm pretty sure that's what your parents were arguing about, though. See—" Rose's eyes glazed over with remembered pain "—your daddy was having one hell of a fling with Gloria. One he never bothered to hide from your poor mama."

Chapter Eight

"An affair?" Tory said, the words coming out in a whisper.

She heard Rose's deep intake of breath as her head swirled with vague images of her father.

"Look," Rose said, her voice firm, "just because your father was carrying on with a tramp like Gloria, it doesn't mean he didn't love your mama."

Tory felt her mouth fall open as she gaped at Rose.

The other woman's expression became a mixture of guilt and cynicism. "Your father was nothing like my useless ex-husband, of course. Joe Don left me and the boys. Your father *never* would have left your mama for *that* woman."

"Is that why you think she was the one who killed Daddy?"

Rose's expression suddenly became unreadable. She shrugged and started the engine before she finally answered, "I don't *know* anything. Not for certain, at least."

"But you think it's a possibility?" she pressed.

"It's a possibility that I was the killer," Rose said philosophically. "Or any of the others who worked for your dad. Hell, for all I know, it could have been Grif. They were close fishing buddies.''

"Grif and my father were friends? I thought he was just a customer.''

"He's been at the restaurant every Friday and Saturday night for nearly twenty years.'' Rose smiled as she added, "I kinda hoped he'd get lost when Shelby and I turned it in to a fancier place and filled it with ferns.''

Tory felt the corners of her lips begin to tug into a grin. "I remember when it was the Rusty Nail. Brewster didn't do much to it while he owned it, but you and Shelby have turned it into a pretty swank place.''

"And renovating the dependency will only make things better.''

"Only if your son manages to maintain the historical feel of the building. When people dine in the Tattoo, they have the sense that they're dinner guests in a home back in the nineteenth century.''

"J.D. knows what we want done,'' Rose defended.

Tory heard the trace of maternal anger in her employer's voice and decided to shut up.

"And Lord knows the city and the historical society have given him enough grief that he wouldn't dare do anything to jeopardize the project or the zillions of permits, title searches and letters of approval he's been working on for the past few weeks.''

They reached the Rose Tattoo before the beginning of lunch service. Tory watched as Chad struggled with the heavy back door. His high-pitched little voice chanted a singsong version of the word *hello*. Since, at his young age, Chad had yet to master consonant sounds, many of his l's came out as w's, making him sound like Elmer Fudd.

"Hi, sweetie," Tory said as she scooped the small boy into her arms to receive a tight hug from his pudgy little arms.

Dylan appeared instantly, his eyes fixed on his son. "You must not try to open the back door," he scolded.

Dylan's stern voice only served to tighten Chad's hold on Tory. He resisted when Dylan reached for him, clutching her as Dylan claimed the wriggling child.

"Noooo!" Chad cried.

"Yes," Dylan insisted. "You'll have to sit in your chair for five minutes for breaking the rules."

"Noooo!" Chad said more emphatically. His small legs began to kick at Dylan's body. "No chair."

Dylan turned and anchored the flailing child on his hip, speaking over his shoulder. "His mother believes in 'time outs.' My mother believed in the back of her hand. I'm beginning to see the wisdom in my mother's method."

Tory swallowed her laughter.

Dylan held the door for them with his foot as Chad changed tactics and began a soft whimper.

The kitchen was a maze of gleaming stainless steel with a full variety of dishes in various stages of preparation. The aroma of freshly chopped herbs competed with the scents of roasting meats and baked goods.

Tory's stomach responded almost instantly, churning and gurgling to remind her that it had been much too long since her last meal. She was about to move toward the setup counter to steal a few olives, when

Rose stopped her by placing her hand at the center of her back.

"Come upstairs with me."

Reluctantly, and with a hand flattened against her empty stomach, Tory followed Rose up the narrow staircase that led to the second story.

The upstairs level had been her home, yet with the many changes made, she didn't get that sense of nostalgia that came with homecoming. Bedrooms were now offices, and the windows, although they resembled the originals, were now double-paned and energy-efficient replicas, which completely eliminated the drafts of hot and cold air she had battled as a child.

On hot days like today, the heat would have warmed the worn wooden floor and the air would have been stifling between the infrequent cross breezes. Every door and window would have been opened in a vain attempt to keep the large home cool while the kitchen below added to the heat.

Shelby was behind her desk, her chair pushed back to accommodate her ever-increasing abdomen. She greeted them with a half smile, probably because Chad's pleas for leniency could be heard through the thin wall.

"How did it go?" Shelby asked.

"We found the perfect dresses," Rose answered enthusiastically. "The last cog in the wheel is having Susan get her fanny down to Faye's shop."

Tory, who stood lingering in the doorway of what was once her parents' bedroom, simply listened as Rose continued to ramble.

Rose turned sideways, her eyes finding Tory. The woman's expression indicated that a new detail had entered her head—one that wasn't making her too happy.

"What are we going to do about having you escorted down the aisle?"

"Escorted?" Tory parroted.

Rose's expression moved off to visit her wandering thoughts.

Shelby stood, stretching as she got to her feet. "It won't actually be an aisle, more like the tables arranged so that there's a walkway between the front door and the fireplace."

Tory held up both hands, her head shaking as she tried to digest this sudden turn of events.

"The wedding is going to happen here?" she asked.

"You bet," Rose chimed in. "We're closing down for the whole day and doing it right."

"You're closing the restaurant on a Friday?" Tory asked. "But that's one of our busiest nights and, besides—" she paused to take a deep breath "—J.D. and I can just track down a justice of the pe—"

"Not on your life," Rose interrupted. "Now that Wesley is coming, I want to show off this place. What better way than to host a private affair like a wedding with all the trimmings? We'll decorate the fireplace with candles, flowers and ribbons. It will make a stunning altar."

"Rose." Tory heard caution in Shelby's tone. "I'm getting a sense here that you didn't discuss any of this with Tory. I've just spent the morning canceling all our reservations for Friday and Tory looks like she's about to scream."

"You don't mind, do you?" Rose asked, giving Tory her full attention. "J.D. said it would be fine. He gave me the green light to handle the arrangements. He said anything I decided was okay with him.''

"I suppose I just wasn't expecting anything quite this elaborate. Our wedding being so... sudden.''

"If I wasn't married and I met a man like J.D....'' Shelby smiled wistfully. "Believe me, I know what it's like to fall hard in the first ten minutes. I hadn't known Dylan more than a few seconds before he swept me off my feet.''

"She's leaving out the fact that I picked her up because there was glass on the floor and she was barefoot at the time,'' Dylan commented as he joined them, carrying a red-eyed Chad. Faint stains of frustrated tears still dampened the little boy's cheeks and he was sucking in short, dramatic little breaths.

"Dylan's such a romantic,'' Shelby grumbled to Tory.

"He needs a nap,'' Dylan said as he moved next to his wife. "And so do you,'' he added to Shelby.

Chad thrust himself toward his mother, only to have the move countered easily by Dylan's strong hold. "You can take a nap with Mommy,'' he soothed his son. "But you're too big for her to carry right now.''

"Actually,'' Shelby said as she placed a kiss on Chad's cheek, "I'm the one who's too big.''

Chad giggled and said, "Fat,'' pointing to his mother's stomach.

"You'll be a real charmer when you grow up,'' Shelby returned as she slung her tiny purse over her shoulder. "You'd better start having those father-son talks with him, Dylan. You know, a male-bonding opportunity where you explain to him why he should never call a lady fat.''

"I'll work on it,'' Dylan replied.

"Speaking of male activities," Rose chimed up, looking directly at Tory. "We still need to find someone to walk you down the aisle."

"Grif," Tory answered without really thinking it through.

"The lush who's in here every weekend?" came a deep voice from directly behind her.

Tory started at the unexpected appearance of J.D., then offered him a wilting look for sneaking up on her and for his nasty remark about Grif.

"Grif isn't a lush, he's a regular."

"A regular alcoholic," J.D. retorted dryly.

Tory and J.D. stepped out of the way of the Tanner family as soon as all the appropriate goodbyes were said. It wasn't long before she felt J.D.'s eyes on her, his face clearly registering his dismay as he took in the easily discernible outline of her body. The intensity of his perusal made her feel almost naked, and she struggled to repress her sudden urge to cover up.

"All set for lunch?" he asked, his voice slightly hoarse.

"Definitely," she said. Taking in his attire, Tory felt a tad overdressed in her skirt and blouse. If he hadn't already announced that he had rented a tux for the ceremony, she would have sworn the man wore nothing but faded jeans and neatly pressed cotton shirts. The shirt he had selected for their "date" was emerald green and managed to compliment her outfit as if they'd somehow coordinated their efforts. *As if they were a couple,* her traitorous thoughts taunted.

"I need to go by my apartment," she said, unable to meet his eyes.

"For what?"

"To change," she answered in a barely audible voice.

"You don't need to change. You're dressed perfectly for the restaurant I have in mind. And," he added, bending forward so that Rose could not hear his words, "I think you look great dressed as a girl."

Her temper simmered but she kept her mouth clamped shut. Though she knew he was teasing, it didn't keep her from feeling annoyed with his comment. It seemed as if this was the day when her anatomy was going to be the chief topic of every conversation, and there wasn't a damned thing she could do about it.

"Where are you taking her?" Rose asked, her expression gleeful as her palms rubbed together excitedly. Apparently, she already knew about and approved of this date idea.

"WaHoo! Grill and Raw Bar," he told his mother. "Susan told me the local cuisine would be good for my karma."

"I can't believe you took a recommendation from Susan," Rose responded. "The girl isn't capable of using both lobes of her brain on the same day."

"The food there is really good," Tory spoke up. It wasn't so much that she felt Susan needed defending, since Rose's assessment of the other waitress was right on, but that she had a hunch Susan had recommended the place to J.D. because she knew it was one of Tory's favorite spots. All that stuff about karma was just flavoring.

"Well," Rose said with a sigh, "I guess I best get downstairs and make sure everything is ready for the lunch crowd." She smoothed her hair and moved toward the door. "You two enjoy yourselves."

Tory wanted to tell her boss that she didn't think that was possible. All of a sudden, the mere thought of being on a date with J.D. had every nerve in her body tingling with some sort of undefined anticipation, mixed with a healthy dose of hesitancy.

HE FOLLOWED HER down the staircase, his eyes riveted to the way the brown skirt outlined her shapely figure. His body began to respond in a most embarrassing fashion as he escorted her to his waiting car. When he slipped behind the wheel, he almost moaned from the discomfort and his inability to do anything about it.

"Did you find a dress?"

"Yes."

"Did Rose pick it out or did you?"

"It was my decision."

"Did they give you a selection to choose from?"

Tory was apparently growing impatient with his interrogation. He could see her stiff posture and that slight narrowing of her eyes when he gave a quick glance in her direction before starting the car and pulling into traffic.

"I have a damn wedding gown, J.D. And in case you care, it cost more than my first car."

"Did I ask how much it cost?"

"No."

"Then don't make an issue out of it, doll."

"If you have so much money to spend on this sham of a wedding, why won't you just lend me the money to finish school and we can forget this whole marriage thing?"

"I've already explained that. You have no collateral, and, in case you haven't noticed, this 'sham of a wedding', as you so eloquently put it, is making Rose immensely happy.''

"If you're so hell-bent on making her happy, why don't you try calling her Mom instead of Rose?'' Tory asked. "Can't you see the pain in her eyes every time you call her by name?''

One hand remained on the wheel while the other balled into a fist and gave the steering wheel a minor punch. "Do us both a favor, Tory. Spare me your well-intentioned insights into my dysfunctional relationship with Rose. I get enough of that crap from Wes.''

"It isn't crap,'' she argued. "We're two intelligent adults about to do something very crazy and very stupid. Even Susan wouldn't be irresponsible enough to marry a complete stranger.''

"It's a done deal, doll,'' he said, expelling a breath.

In the ensuing silence, J.D. didn't know whether to be angry at her for continually insisting that all he had to do was call Rose "Mom'' and give her a big kiss, in order for all those years of childhood pain to go away. Or, maybe, he was feeling annoyed because he couldn't kiss Tory. Her mouth had become something of a fixation lately. He imagined the soft, pliant moistness of her lips, anticipated the sweet, almost naive response. He dreamed about it—thought about kissing her when he was supposed to be working. Hell, when he should have been watching the crew begin work around the dependency, he stood watching the kitchen window, hoping to catch an occasional glimpse of her as she worked. It wasn't making any sense, this fierce curiosity he felt for Tory on every level. Physically, it was killing him to keep his hands off her. But there was more to it than that. He just didn't know yet what that "more'' was.

"This is *your* favorite place?" he asked in a surprised tone when he was handed a menu and read the eclectic selections, many of which had a distinctive Caribbean flare—conch fritters and chowder, mango salsa. It was almost like being back home. He missed his home, but he was also beginning to wonder how much he would miss Tory when she found out the truth.

"I've never had a bad meal here, and it's a nice change from the traditional southern-fried specialties."

The soft lighting in the room illuminated the shimmering fire in her eyes. It was like looking at a professionally done photograph. Her skin was flawless, shadows appearing on her high cheekbones from her thick, feathery lashes. Her menu was in the defensive position, what he now recognized as her way of making sure no one noticed her ample figure.

"Have you decided?" the waiter asked.

"I'm still thinking," J.D. told him. Of course, his first choice was to drag Tory across the table and kiss her until she couldn't see straight. Unfortunately, she definitely wasn't an entrée.

"I ran a few errands while you were out with Rose," he said as he poured wine into each of their glasses.

"Does this mean I can count on you to go to the dry cleaners and do the shopping after we're married?" she teased.

He grinned. "Don't push it. Anyway, we have full laundry service at the condo. Cleaning service, too."

"The condo? We?"

"You didn't think I would move into your place, did you?"

He watched as she brought the glass to her lips and drained nearly half of the Chablis. "I guess I hadn't really thought about it."

"I think you'll find my place comfortable. It's closer to Oglethorpe College, but a little farther away from your mother."

That veil of sadness fell across her face at the mere mention of her mother.

"But with your reduced work schedule, I'll make sure you see her whenever you want."

"What reduced work schedule?"

"Rose is going to cut back your hours and hire another waitress to pick up the slack."

He found the flash of anger in her eyes almost amusing. "I only suggested it because I was under the impression that you wanted some hands-on experience with renovating the dependency." J.D. leaned back in his chair, taking his wineglass with him. "But if you'd rather wait tables . . ."

The anger vanished and she became as excited as a child seeing her first new bicycle on Christmas morning. "You really are going to let me work with you?"

"*For* me," he corrected, his expression growing solemn. "I know you have an impressive academic record when it comes to old buildings, but I suspect you haven't been around too much actual construction. I'll expect you to follow my directions, even when you don't agree with them, just like any other employee."

Tory gave him a salute. "Sir, yes sir."

"Cute," he mocked. "But I'm serious. You'll be allowed to work on the project as long as you behave."

J.D. winced as the final word crossed his lips. It was instantly apparent that Tory hadn't taken well to the use of that particular condescension. Since he could think of no graceful way to back out of his blunder, he opted to summon the waiter, order their food and change the subject.

"I found out who Evan Richards is," he said.

"The guy who Detective Greer mentioned this morning?"

J.D. nodded just as the waiter placed a steaming, fragrant bowl of conch chowder in front of him. "He's a CPA. Has a decent-size office in Summerville."

"What did he have to do with my father?"

"I don't know yet, but I thought you might like to take a drive up there and ask him after lunch."

Chapter Nine

Summerville was a bedroom community far removed from the historic part of the city. It was a maze of lovely developments where swing sets and gas grills were standard issue. It did have a small business district, which is where they found the offices of Evan Richards.

Tory was impressed. Evan's accounting firm occupied both floors of the large, custom-designed building.

"Looks like the guy's doing pretty well for himself," J.D. commented as he held the door for her.

"I bet your offices make this place look like a converted garage," she retorted.

"You'll find out soon enough," he answered as they approached the receptionist's desk.

Yeah, right, Tory thought, though she decided not to call him on it.

A well-groomed woman, who appeared to be about Tory's age, offered a welcoming smile. Actually, Tory amended, she offered J.D. the smile—Tory she barely noticed.

"Can I help you?" she asked from behind a highly polished oval desk.

"We'd like to see Mr. Richards," J.D. answered.

The woman looked down, then up at them, her face perplexed. "Mr. Richards doesn't have any appointments scheduled for this afternoon."

"We don't have an appointment," J.D. told her.

"I see," she said with a nod. "I'd be happy to let you see his secretary, perhaps she can—"

"Mr. Richards is an old friend of my family's," Tory interjected. "When I saw his name on the sign outside, I just thought it would be nice if I dropped in to say a quick hello."

The excuse appeared to appease the woman, since she grabbed the phone and called some person named Margaret. After repeating Tory's lie, she covered the mouthpiece and asked, "Your name?"

"Victoria Conway."

A flicker of morbid curiosity passed across the woman's face. Apparently, she'd been reading the newspaper accounts of the remains of Bob Conway recently discovered in the dependency. The receptionist passed along the information to Margaret, then waited a few moments before saying to them, "Take the elevator up to the second floor. Mr. Richards's office is at the far end to the left."

As soon as the elevator doors slid closed, J.D. said, "You're a fairly decent little fibber, doll."

"I didn't actually lie," she corrected. "I simply omitted the fact that we drove out here specifically to see him." Crossing her arms in front of her, Tory stood rigidly still as J.D. reached around her to depress the illuminated button marked with the number two. His forearm brushed her side for just a fraction of a second, but it was enough to cause tiny sparks of vivid awareness to start racing through her veins.

His scent filled the small elevator compartment, tantalizing her further. How was she going to handle living in the same house with this man? And why did he have this almost magical ability to make her wonder how it would feel to be locked in his arms? Would his kisses be as demanding as the man himself?

"Are you waiting for some sort of invitation?" J.D. asked as he placed one large hand at the small of her back and nudged her from the elevator.

"I was just lost in thought for a minute," she told him testily, swatting his hand away.

"Do you remember this Richards character?"

Tory shook her head. "Maybe when I see him."

The plush carpeting drowned out the sounds of their footsteps. Unfortunately, it did nothing to quiet the sound of her heart beating in her ears. She had to stop thinking such provocative thoughts about J.D. Her curiosity was becoming far too intense, not to mention the way he'd wormed himself into her dreams. If this marriage thing was going to work, she was definitely going to have to find some way to shut off the flood of raging hormones.

Evan's office was decorated in what she could only call "Early Roadkill." Sundry dead creatures were mounted on every wall, their glass eyes staring down from above. She shivered as she stepped over the spotted rug of some poor creature's hide and introduced herself to the secretary who she assumed was Margaret.

The attractive brunette told them to have a seat, then disappeared behind a door marked Private.

J.D. sprawled on the zebra-striped sofa, while Tory opted for one of the high-backed leather chairs in front of a small coffee table. Actually, it wasn't a coffee table, but a Plexiglas rectangle that housed yet another collection of stuffed and posed critters. She found the display more disgusting than Rose's authentic Elvis Presley toenail.

Leaning forward was a mistake for two reasons. First, the magazine selection dealt only with hunting, fishing, guns and rifles. Second, she was immediately aware that J.D.'s eyes had wandered over to peek down the front of her blouse. She should have reprimanded him for such a childish action, but for some unexplainable reason, she continued to thumb through the titles. She had always shied away from allowing men to ogle her body, yet a large part of her was thrilled to think that this man found her appealing.

"Victoria!"

She shot out of the chair at the unfamiliar voice calling her name.

"Mr. Richards," she said in an unusually husky voice. A remnant, no doubt, of a J.D. fantasy interrupted.

"Evan, please," he said in a smooth, cultured southern accent. He held out both hands, taking hers as he stood back for a long appraisal of her. "You certainly have changed a good deal since the last time I saw you."

His attention moved back to her face, and she noticed instantly that he wasn't making eye contact. Then she remembered her companion.

She introduced J.D. to the short, lean man. J.D.'s larger hand swallowed Evan's for a quick handshake.

Evan ushered them into his office, where, unfortunately, the dead-animal motif was continued. Separating the various stuffed beasts was a variety of wall plaques, awards and a single photograph. It was the photograph that caught her eye.

Evan was standing next to a large winch from which dangled a huge fish—the same huge fish mounted and hanging behind his mahogany desk. On the opposite side of the fish was another man—Grif. And, she thought as she tried not to be too obvious in her study, the picture was fairly recent.

"Sit, sit," Evan said, waving his arm in the general direction of the comfortable chairs angled toward his clutter-free desktop.

"So," he began, speaking mainly to J.D., "I can't tell you how shocked I was when I read about Bob's body being found at the Rusty Nail."

"Rose Tattoo," Tory corrected. "The new owners have changed the place. You'd probably like it. It's upscale and the food is superb."

Evan seemed taken aback by her endorsement. Blotting small beads of perspiration from his upper lip with what looked to be an expensive linen handkerchief, he forced a smile. "I don't get into town very often."

"Too busy hunting and fishing?" J.D. asked, making absolutely no attempt to keep the contempt from his question.

Evan didn't immediately react to J.D.'s tone. He was too preoccupied in growing more nervous by the second. Faint perspiration stains were beginning to form beneath the armpits of his monogrammed shirt.

"I enjoy sporting," he said slightly defensively. "I take it you aren't a sportsman, Mr. Porter."

"Never got into it myself," J.D. answered easily as he crossed one leg over the other. "I don't see much sport in camouflaging myself in the woods with a high-powered gun at my side. Now, if you tell me you got all these kills by chasing the animal down and hitting it with a rock, then I'll be impressed.''

Evan's round face took on the distinctive red hue of barely contained anger. Tory took in a breath and expelled it slowly. She then placed her hand on J.D.'s knee. She felt him start at the contact and saw, out of the corner of her eye, his surprised expression. The surprise multiplied when she stabbed her fingernails into the taut tendons on either side of his knee.

"You'll have to forgive J.D., Evan. I'm sure he didn't mean to preach." Pulling her hand away from J.D. she continued, "He's just one of those people who can't keep their opinions to themselves." She gave J.D. a fast reprimand with her eyes before turning back to their host.

Evan appeared to relax a bit. At least he stopped dabbing at his upper lip. But the stains beneath his arms seemed to continue to grow and spread. "No offense taken," he said.

"You have a lovely office," Tory managed to say with a straight face. "And you must have had an excellent architect. The building is so... distinctive."

Evan beamed. "Henderson did the design."

"Greg Henderson?" J.D. asked.

"Yes. Do you know him?"

"Only professionally. Trade shows, that sort of thing," J.D. answered, his tone now civil.

"You're an architect?" Evan asked, scratching his scalp through perfectly styled brown hair.

"Down in Miami."

"He's up here to help Rose and Shelby renovate the dependency behind the Tattoo."

"So that's how they discovered the...."

"Remains," Tory supplied, hoping to get the man past his discomfort. "I was wondering what you did for my father back when he owned the place."

Evan shrugged. "I balanced the books," he said, a faintly disapproving smile curled his lips. "Your father wasn't one of my easiest clients. He had a difficult time maintaining good records."

"You had other clients besides Tory's father?" J.D. asked.

The redness returned. "Not a lot," he admitted. "I was just starting out back then. Building my client base."

"So you only handled the bar?" J.D. pressed.

Evan nodded. "Except for tax time. Then I did a little free-lancing."

She watched as J.D. stroked his chin thoughtfully. "I was given to believe that you had been working for one of those franchise tax-return joints before you took on the Rusty Nail."

Evan's redness evolved into a drained paleness and out came the handkerchief again. "I did a lot of things back then, Mr. Porter. Who doesn't when they're fresh out of college?"

"I know what you mean," J.D. agreed. "But I don't understand how you could have afforded to leave the franchise joint to take on a single client who had no business skills. Tough to pay the bills that way."

"I told you," Evan said, his voice increasing in volume. "I supplemented my income by doing 1040s. And who are you to come in here asking about my background?" He turned angry brown eyes on Tory. "You told my receptionist that this was a friendly visit. It feels more like an interrogation."

"I'm sorry, Evan. But surely you can understand that I'm interested in my father's life prior to his murder. This has all been something of a shock for me."

"So you bring along this gorilla to intimidate me?" Evan countered.

"If I were a gorilla, you'd probably be thrilled," J.D. interjected. "Then you could take aim, kill me and have me stuffed and mounted. As it happens, Tory is my fiancée, which should explain my presence."

"Congratulations," Evan muttered. "But I can't be of any help to you. I only worked for Bob Conway for a year or so, and it was a long time ago."

"Can you tell me anything about a woman named Gloria?" Tory asked.

Evan hesitated, then nodded slowly and said, "I believe there was a waitress by that name at the Rusty Nail."

"I was told she was more than just a waitress."

Her bluntness apparently caught him off guard. "There were rumors," he said, obviously choosing his words carefully.

Tory frowned at him. "Rumors, or a blatant affair?"

Pinching the bridge of his nose, Evan sucked in a gulp of air and nodded. "They were pretty open about the whole thing. It was really pathetic."

"How so?" J.D. asked.

"Tory," Evan said in a pleading voice, "do you think dredging up all this old unpleasantness is really necessary?"

"It won't bring my father back, Evan. But it might tell me who killed him."

"While we're on the subject," J.D. said, uncrossing his legs and leaning forward. "Did you kill him?"

"J.D.!"

"Of all the nerve," Evan bellowed. His cheeks puffed out to match those of the fish mounted behind him. "I don't—" The buzz of the intercom cut him off and he picked up the receiver. "Give me five minutes," Evan instructed his secretary, then slammed the receiver back into place.

Pushing himself away from the desk, Evan stood, his posture indicating their dismissal. "It seems there is a police officer here to interview me, so I believe we'll have to conclude our reunion."

"I'm really sorry if we upset you, Evan," Tory said as she got up. "Grif will no doubt chew me out when he finds out J.D. and I came here and wasted your time."

"Yes," Evan began, clearing his throat before continuing. "I'll leave your reprimanding to Grif. He always has been better at that sort of thing. I wish you well in your marriage," he added almost as an afterthought.

"I wish you well with Detective Greer," J.D. countered. "For some strange reason, he's hell-bent on solving this case."

They left Evan panting and pale. Out in the anteroom, Greer's reaction was a different matter. He seemed amazed when he saw them. Then he appeared to get a tad perturbed. "I thought you had no interest in finding your father's killer," he stated.

"She never said she had no interest," J.D. corrected. "She just told you that finding the culprit wouldn't bring back her father."

Greer glared at him. J.D. was beginning to understand why Rose so disliked this guy. He reminded J.D. of one of those small, annoying breeds of dogs—the kind that nipped at your ankles.

"Either help me or don't," the detective told Tory. "But don't get in my way. Or have you already talked to Griffen and Matthews?"

"Cal Matthews?" he heard Tory ask.

J.D. thought he heard something in her voice—recognition, perhaps?

With a grunt of pure annoyance, Greer flipped through his notebook until he found a particular page. "Right, Calvin Matthews. Currently he owns—"

"Cal's Place on Market Street," Tory said. "He used to work for my father. I remember him being there all the time when I was little. He's been visiting my mother on and off over the years."

"Selective memory?" Greer sneered. "Or are you suddenly feeling cooperative?"

J.D. stepped between Tory and the police official, his hands balled in tight fists by his sides. "You seem to have trouble remembering she was just a kid when all this happened. Is *that* selective memory or are you just too lazy to do your own legwork?"

"Stop it," Tory told him at the same time he felt her small fingers wrap around his arm.

It was his undoing. It was a little hard to maintain his anger at the detective with the feel of her soft, delicate hand touching him. Sidestepping Greer as if the man were a pile of animal excrement, J.D. took hold of Tory's hand and walked her past the detective, straight to the elevator. Thanks to his residual anger, he punched the button with extra force.

"Are you always so confrontational?"

He waited for the elevator doors to close before offering his answer. He still held tightly to her hand. "Did you think I was just going to stand there and let him talk to you like that?"

"Not Greer," she said, jerking her arm, but making no effort to pull away from him. "I was talking about Evan."

"The Great White Sweating Hunter?"

He heard her soft laughter and it had an amazingly calming effect on his system.

"Your old friend Evan is a liar."

"You should be marrying Susan on Friday," she suggested. "Apparently, you two share the gift of psychic communication."

He let her little taunt pass as they made their way to his car. When they reached the passenger side, J.D. turned her gently, his palms resting on her shoulders, his eyes locked on hers. "I'm not marrying anyone but you on Friday, doll. Understand?"

He watched as a faint blush painted her high cheekbones. "It w-was a joke," she stammered.

"Well, I just wanted to make sure you understood that the wedding will take place on Friday. Period."

Her eyes narrowed as her annoyance came to life. "I've already said yes. I have a dress. You have a tux. What part of this wedding *haven't* I cooperated with?"

"This part," he said as his hands moved over the silken skin of her neck, tilting her head back to receive his kiss.

Chapter Ten

"Now, now," she said as she ducked out of his grasp. "Don't you know it's bad luck to kiss the bride before the ceremony?"

J.D. allowed his arms to fall limply to his sides, his nostrils still filled with the scent of her perfume, his memory etched with the silken feel of her skin. Forcing a smile to his lips, he responded, "I believe the tradition is that I'm not supposed to *see* the bride before the ceremony."

"Well, since this isn't exactly a traditional marriage, I thought it would be okay to make up a few things along the way."

Several minutes later, J.D. found himself pulling onto the expressway and wondering why Tory had rebuked his attempt to kiss her. It wasn't a normal rejection, he thought as he melded into the steady stream of late-day traffic. He sensed she was as curious about him as he was about her; yet something was holding her back.

His conclusion was confirmed when he turned to take a quick look at her profile. She looked content, almost happy. Hardly the behavior of a woman disgusted by a man's attempt at an ordinary kiss. *Ordi-*

nary kiss, his brain repeated sarcastically. Something told him kissing Tory would be a lot of things—and ordinary wasn't one of them.

"Where are we going?"

"I thought you might like to see my place since you'll be moving in after Friday." He could almost feel the tension begin to stiffen her small body. Battling to keep his attention on driving, J.D. decided he might as well tell her about all the arrangements. *No,* his conscience piped up. What he should be doing is telling her the truth.

"I've arranged for a moving company to get the stuff out of your apartment next week. They'll take it to a storage place near the airport."

"You did what?" she wailed.

"My condo is furnished," he told her. "And a whole hell of a lot better than your yard-sale decor."

"But those are my personal belongings. What gives you the right to place my things in storage without checking with me first?" she demanded indignantly. "You and your mother are really starting to get on my nerves, J.D. First, I'm railroaded into a marriage. Instead of a simple exchange of lies in front of a justice of the peace, I'm having the wedding of the century. Now, you tell me I'm not even going to have access to my own stuff?"

He let out a slow, calming breath. This woman's temper was the last thing he wanted to deal with. He was having a hard enough time dealing with his own frustrations. "You're welcome to bring anything to the condo you want."

"Gee, thanks," she retorted. "Will I also be given one half of one dresser drawer?"

He laughed aloud, which didn't seem to sit too well with his companion. "There's plenty of room for anything and everything you want to bring with you. Except," he said as he veered off an exit into a tree-lined suburb, "that damned sofa of yours goes into storage. It's more uncomfortable than it is ugly, and that's a phenomenal accomplishment."

"Sorry my furniture doesn't meet with your approval. Perhaps I should call Evan and ask him the name of *his* decorator."

"It would be more productive if you asked him how he managed such a smooth and speedy rise to his present professional status."

"Meaning?"

J.D. whipped the Mercedes into one of the spots reserved for his unit. "Before he had that fancy building built, he rented some pricey office space downtown."

"How do you know?"

"I asked Dylan to check the guy out for me."

"An alcohol, tobacco and firearms agent has nothing better to do than look into the life and times of a harmless accountant?"

Cutting the engine, J.D. turned to take in her innocent expression. "What makes you think he's harmless? The guy's office looks like a sick version of a wax petting zoo. An avid hunter doesn't find it hard to pull a trigger."

He felt a twinge of regret at the harshness of his words when she visibly blanched.

"I see your point." She reached for the door handle and J.D. wished he could do something to erase the pain he'd seen in her eyes. He was already beginning to imagine the pain he would cause when she eventually learned the truth.

SHE COULD HAVE described where he lived even before she stepped foot in the spacious condo overlooking Charleston Harbor. It was one of those sterile-looking places—all open spaces, stark white walls and white furniture. Tory made a mental note to invite Chad over for a chocolate ice-cream cone as soon as she was in residence.

"You don't like it," J.D. said before his lips pulled into a tight line.

"What's not to like?" she answered, moving forward to take in the magnificent view of the water and the Charleston skyline beyond. "It must be beautiful at night," she murmured when she sensed he'd come up behind her. "I can even see Fort Sumter from here," she said with genuine enthusiasm.

"It has a great kitchen," he said, his breath warm where it washed across the exposed skin of her neck.

Tory felt her pulse quicken and knew it was imperative that she put some space between herself and J.D. The temptation to touch him was nearly overwhelming. "Show it to me," she suggested as she sidestepped the big man.

He was right. It was a great kitchen, with every modern convenience, including a built-in grill and a warming oven. "You've got a better setup here than we have at the Tattoo," she teased. "Rose must have been blown away when she saw this."

"She's never been here," he said in a voice devoid of emotion.

Tory met and held his silver eyes. "Inviting your mother over for dinner is a crime in your book?"

His expression hardened. "There just hasn't been an opportunity."

"Yet," Tory said with a satisfied smile. "I'll enjoy inviting my boss to dinner once I'm mistress of this sterile abode."

J.D. matched her expression with a lopsided smirk. He took a step forward so that he loomed above her, mere inches separating them. "Since you used the word mistress, I guess that means I can look forward to coming home to elegantly prepared dishes from my *mistress.*"

The emphasis he placed on the last word made her blush from the roots of her hair to the tips of her toes. She made a mental note to pay stricter attention to her word choices. "Show me the rest of the place," she stated in an uncharacteristically high-pitched voice.

J.D. led her down the hallway, pointing out a linen closet and powder room along the way. "This is my office," he said as he pushed open the door and flipped a switch on the wall to combat the growing darkness.

"Wow," was all she could manage to say when she moved in to admire the state-of-the-art setup. The drafting table was neatly arranged with the tools of his trade. And the computer station was like something out of a science-fiction novel. "Does it have CAD?" she asked as she walked over to the computer.

"The latest version," he said as he reached over and pushed the "on" button.

In no time at all, she was treated to a full-color version of the computer-aided design program that she had only read about in magazines and journals.

"Wanna see what I've come up with so far?"

"For the dependency?" she asked, her eyes still riveted to the screen as she sat in the padded rolling chair in front of the machine.

J.D. reached around her and Tory felt the hardness of well-defined muscle press against her back. Her body was electrified where it touched his. The soft mat of dark hair on his forearms tickled as his large fingers worked nimbly on the keyboard. He had a scent all his own, heady and masculine—and incredibly distracting.

Tory forced her attention straight ahead to the image filling the screen. She didn't find it nearly as interesting as the gentle brush of his face against her earlobe. The room felt suddenly warm, a stark contrast to the clammy dampness of her palms as she flattened them against the front of her skirt. She remembered Evan's telltale sweat stains and jerked her hands away from her clothing.

In the process, she managed to give J.D. a decent whack in the jaw with the back of her head.

"Sorry," she said as complete humiliation overcame budding desire. "One of those muscle spasms, I guess."

"No harm done," he said, reaching around her and continuing his work.

Tory squirmed in the chair as he showed her the various renovations in different dimensions and scale. Normally, she would have been riveted by the impressive computer program. However, normal didn't seem to apply where J.D. was concerned. Not in the way she was so cognizant of the fluid motions of his body, the deep, soothing tone of his voice.

"This has been great," she said, pushing away from the computer and rolling over his foot in the process. "Oops."

"Now I know why they say most accidents happen in the home," he grunted as he hopped on one leg, rubbing his injured instep.

"I'm not usually this klutzy," she told him, her eyes downcast.

"You're nervous. I understand."

Never had she been the recipient of such kindness. It was in the deep gray of his eyes, in the sexy half smile on his lips. What should have made her feel better only magnified her own awkwardness. Suddenly, Tory was conscious of herself in a whole new way. Somehow, things like posture, her hair, her skirt length—it all seemed to matter. She knew immediately it was time for a change in venue.

"So show me the rest of this place."

"The only room left is the bedroom," he told her, his eyes fixed on hers.

Tory swallowed, then forced a smile to her lips. "This place came with a bedroom? What will they think of next." Her humor seemed to short-circuit the currents flowing between them as she followed him into the adjacent room.

Of course, the electricity came flooding back the instant she caught a glimpse of the huge bed dominating the room. Immediately, she averted her eyes, fixing her gaze on what she could see of the bathroom.

"It comes with a pool, too," she quipped as she walked into the bathroom and moved to run her fingers along the smooth, cool tiles of the first step leading up to a deep, more-than-one-person Jacuzzi.

Tilting her head back slightly, she grinned and asked, "What, no diving board?"

"They only come with the three-bedroom models."

Wrapped in the warmth of good humor, Tory and J.D. made their way back to the kitchen. He directed her to one of the bar stools while he moved to the refrigerator.

After rummaging a bit, he appeared from behind the door balancing the ingredients for a salad and two steaks.

"You cook?" she asked with mock exaggeration.

"PBS won't be giving me my own show, but I get by. Before I forget," J.D. said as soon as he had placed the food on top of the center island, "here's a card for you to use, and our flight leaves at eight o'clock Saturday morning."

Accepting the credit card, Tory nearly gasped when she read the name stamped in the plastic—Victoria Porter. "Why do I need a credit card? And what flight? Going where?"

J.D. didn't say anything at first, he rinsed mushrooms instead. "You can charge anything you might need for our..."

"Honeymoon?" Tory suggested, saying the word as if it had just then been invented.

"Yeah," he grumbled as he savagely chopped the poor vegetables into bits and pieces.

"To where?" she asked, dazed. Then amended her question before he answered. "Why are we going on a honeymoon?"

"It would look sort of strange if we didn't."

"It already looks strange," she told him pointedly. "Wasting good money on—"

"It's a gift from my father and stepmother. Their wedding present."

Tory blinked and said, "Your father and stepmother think you're really getting married?"

He turned then, his eyes shimmering with annoyance. "I am really getting married, Tory. In three days. But then, you should know that since you're the woman I'm marrying."

"I didn't mean it like that," she said, forcing calmness into her tone. "I'm just surprised that you haven't told your family the truth about all this."

"I've told my brother," J.D. said before he went back to his task. "Wes won't breathe a word of any of it to Dad and Shelia."

"Why did you tell him?"

"We're close."

Something about the clipped, two-word response didn't ring true.

"TWO DAYS," she said as she surveyed the clutter in her apartment. In her mind's eye, she pictured J.D.'s place and secretly admitted that it would be a nice change. "And dinner was nice," she continued talking as she began to make piles of things to take and things to leave for storage.

"That's because all we talked about was architecture and preservation," she reminded herself. "Safe subjects." Feeling her eyebrows draw together, Tory tried to fit the puzzle of J.D. in her brain. But there seemed to be too many pieces missing. "Like why are we flying to the Bahamas for a honeymoon on his father and stepmother? Why did he tell his brother the truth and not his father and stepmother?" She reached into her purse and extracted her new credit card. "And how come he won't give me a loan, but he's already gotten me an American Express Gold Card, no less. And why am I talking to—''

The shrill ring of the telephone cut off her monologue. Glancing at her watch, Tory figured it was J.D., who had probably forgotten to tell her they were going to file a joint tax return on top of everything else.

''Hello?''

''Stay out of it,'' the muffled voice mumbled.

''I'm sorry,'' she said, shivering at the creepy-sounding voice. ''You must have the wrong number.''

''I've got the right number, Tory.''

Fear tiptoed up her spine at the sound of her own name. ''Who is this?'' she demanded, trying to stay calm. ''Josh, if this is you, I swear I'll—''

''I'm not the bartender, Tory. I'm just warning you and that boyfriend of yours. The cops will never solve the murder. It would be a shame if something happened to you.''

''Like what?'' she managed to ask, her voice betraying none of the anxiety knotting the pit of her stomach.

''Like a bullet in the back of your head. Just like I did with your father.''

The line went dead and Tory very nearly expired from the memory of the hoarse, menacing voice. Looking down, she noticed her hand, which still held the receiver, was shaking along with the rest of her body.

Slamming the receiver back on the cradle, Tory hugged herself and said, ''It was nothing more than a prank. Some sicko read about the murder in the paper and decided to do something cruel.'' Still, she made a quick run through the apartment, checking every window and door, and even peeking behind the shower curtain and under the bed. She felt more secure and even debated calling J.D. and telling him of the threat. Instead, Tory took the phone off the hook and spent the next several hours sorting, packing and trying to convince herself that she had somehow blown the whole incident out of proportion.

The next morning, she was still bothered by the call and the lack of restful sleep. Dark circles had formed beneath her bloodshot eyes and no amount of cold water splashed on her face lifted that foggy feeling.

After a shower, her whole body still felt heavy as she pulled on a pair of faded denim shorts and a T-shirt with the expression Bad Hair Day emblazoned across the front. It seemed appropriate since she hadn't bothered to blow-dry her hair or apply makeup. After all, she was simply going to make sure the alterations on her wedding dress were correct. Slinging her purse over her shoulder, she had her hand on the doorknob when a knock sounded from the other side.

Normally, she would have opened the door without a thought. However, the creepy call in the wee hours of the morning was still too fresh in her mind. "Who is it?"

"J.D."

"Of course," she grumbled, knowing she couldn't look worse if she tried. She also knew that short of putting a bag over her head, there wasn't a thing she could do to transform herself in the time it took to open a door.

"Tory?" she heard him yell, impatient as ever.

"All right already," she groaned as she yanked open the door.

It was J.D. all right and she didn't need Susan's psychic abilities to know what he thought of her appearance. But it got better and better. To her utter mortification, Tory realized J.D. had brought guests, as well. Judging from the basic physical resemblance of the two men behind J.D., it didn't take her long to realize the Jackass Deluxe had brought the family by without bothering to call.

A tall, willowy blonde who looked close to J.D.'s age stepped forward with more grace and poise than Tory had ever seen.

Extending her hand along with a warm smile, the woman said, "I'm Shelia." Then with a mildly amused look in her pretty green eyes, she added, "But you probably know me better as 'that coed.'"

Tory could feel herself blush. "Nice to meet you," she managed to say with a polite expression, then turned angry eyes up to J.D. "You could have called first," she said through nearly gritted teeth.

"I've been calling all morning. Either your phone is broken or you're worse than a teenager."

"I took it off the hook," Tory admitted.

J.D.'s expression was one of instant concern. "Why?"

"Prank calls last night," she said, averting her eyes. "I just forgot to put it back on the hook when I got up."

"You don't look like you ever went to bed."

"Thanks," she mumbled.

"My brother isn't exactly known for his tact," the youngest man said as he stepped forward. "Or his manners. I'm Wesley Porter, nice to meet you."

He was good, Tory thought as she shook his hand. He knew this whole thing was a sham, but neither his expression nor his actions gave him away. It made her wonder if all the Porter men could lie with such ease.

"And I'm Joseph," the elder Porter said as he stepped forward. He wrapped Tory in his large frame and gave her a tight squeeze. "I can't tell you how happy I am that one of my sons is finally settling down."

Tory couldn't bring herself to say a word. Wesley and J.D. might be capable of deceiving this kind man, but she wasn't up to it.

"Hope there are lots of grandchildren in the plans," he continued.

That's it! Tory thought as she said a silent prayer for a spaceship to fly overhead and remove her from the planet.

"I think we should concentrate on the wedding first," J.D. told his father.

"Speaking of which, I have a fitting for my dress in less than ten minutes." She surveyed the various pairs of curious eyes fixed on her and could only offer an apologetic smile. "You're welcome to stay here," she suggested. "It won't take me too long."

"I'll stay here," J.D. said. Then he reached into his pocket and tossed his car keys to his brother. "We passed the tux place on the way over here. Drop Shelia and Dad at the Omni to shop while you get fitted."

He really did feel sorry for Tory, he thought once he was finally alone in her apartment, which was in complete chaos. The first thing he did was find the phone and put the receiver back on the hook. He shouldn't have brought the family by without warning, but his father had been his usual insistent self. He could only imagine what his father must think of his bride. Tory was attractive, but this morning hadn't exactly been one of her better days. He wondered if she really was getting her dress fitted or if she was off someplace digging a large hole to crawl into. The thought made him smile. So did the lingering scent of her, which filled the dingy apartment.

J.D. had managed his secret mission in her bedroom when he heard a knock at the front door. Careful to step over what he could only assume was some sort of organization system only Tory understood, he answered the knock.

"You're supposed to be renting a tux," he reminded his younger brother.

"Been there, done that," Wes retorted, tossing the keys in the air for J.D. to catch. "I thought I'd keep you company until your bride returns."

"Don't start on me," J.D. warned.

Wesley held up both hands and said, "You're the one who will have to explain all this to Dad when the time comes." He dropped his arms and sat in one of the folding chairs. "Then Dad can be my first patient. I can provide him with grief therapy when he discovers his favorite son lied to him."

"I'm not his favorite," J.D. insisted. "You just suffer from an inferiority complex. Maybe you should be your own first patient. Heal thyself and all that."

"Cute," Wes said with a snicker. "Shelia seems to be taking this pretty well, don't you think?"

"I hadn't thought about it," J.D. admitted. In fact, he thought of little else besides Tory these days. "Why shouldn't she take it well? Rose invited her to the wedding, not pistols at dawn."

"Still haven't gotten past calling her Rose, huh?"

"Go to hell, Wes."

"Or the hostility, either."

"Why don't you go practice your analysis on someone else?" J.D. suggested, tossing a tattered pillow at his brother.

"Because I have so much to work with right here."

"I'm nothing compared to the collection you'll find at the Rose Tattoo," J.D. said with a deep chuckle. "Rose prays at a shrine she's built to Elvis Presley and even makes an annual pilgrimage to Graceland to pay homage. Then there's the bartender, Josh, who sleeps around as if he's trying to commit suicide. Oh…" J.D. paused and shook his head. "Wait until you get a load of the guy Tory has chosen to walk her down the aisle. Thinks he's some sort of cross between Hemingway and the skipper from Gilligan's Island."

Wesley rubbed his hands together excitedly. "A regular psychiatrist's mecca."

"Then there's the palm-reading, karma-counseling waitress. About the only normal people in this whole setup are Shelby and her husband, Dylan. Nice couple. Cute kid, another one on the way."

"Tory isn't normal?" Wes asked in a tone J.D. found as annoying as the way his brother fiddled with the rims of his glasses whenever he asked a "probing" question.

"Of course she's normal," J.D. defended instantly and loudly.

"But?"

"But nothing. She's just not the easiest person in the world to read."

"Translation," his brother said as he pulled the glasses from the bridge of his nose, "you haven't told her the real reason you're marrying her."

Chapter Eleven

"I feel like a real bride," Tory said when Shelby jabbed her with a bobby pin as she continued to secure the simple veil to Tory's professionally coiffed hair.

The remark earned her a stern look of reprimand from Rose.

"You are a real bride," Shelby said. "And you're holding up the start of the ceremony."

Grif, who was leaning against the credenza in the office, looked uncomfortable in his tux. Tory was uncomfortable as she watched him pour himself a third Scotch.

"Stop that," Rose said, taking the glass from the white-haired man. "You can drink yourself into a stupor after the ceremony."

Grif shrugged his acceptance. "You look a lot like your mother did the day she married your father," he observed.

Tory stilled. Looking at Grif through the netting of her veil, she realized that she had almost forgotten that he had attended her parents' wedding.

"Only, your mother wouldn't have let me walk her down the aisle if I were the last man on earth."

"Why not?" Tory asked.

"She thought I drank too much."

"Wonder where she got that notion," Rose mumbled in a stage whisper.

"Well, I'm glad you agreed to escort me," Tory told him. "I've known you my whole life. You were my first and only choice."

Grif blushed at her compliment. "Then I guess we'd best get this show on the road."

"I'll go down and tell them we're ready," Shelby offered. "By the time I take my seat, you should be at the front door."

"I remember," Grif grumbled at her. "We went over all this last night. I drink, but I don't always forget."

"Just be a good boy," Shelby told him in the same tone she used on her young son. "And you," she said as she gave Tory a hug. "I know you're doing the right thing."

"I wish you'd let me take one last look at your palm," Susan said from where she'd been standing quietly and stiffly in the corner. "I'm telling you, Tory. I had a vivid image last night about today. I think maybe you and—"

"I think you'd better shut up," Rose snapped. "You just worry about your own karma and leave Tory and my son alone. This is a wedding, not a 900-psychic line."

"Jeez," Susan muttered. "I am only trying to help."

"Then get downstairs and wait in the alley for your signal," Rose commanded.

Tory and Susan headed for the stairs. After a few minutes had gone by, Tory was marginally aware of a man watching her from the end of the alley, she lifted the hem of her gown to protect it from the layers of dust and dirt on the ground. She probably did look a bit out of place, dressed in her flowing white gown with her arm laced through Grif's, following the procession of Rose and Susan. A bee came to investigate the bouquet of pale pink roses she was carrying and she stopped long enough to swat it away. When she looked up again, the man was gone, probably no longer intrigued by the bride in the alley.

The soft sounds of organ music greeted her as she crossed the checkered threshold at the entrance of the restaurant. Her short walk through the bright sunlight had rendered her nearly blind, a condition further exacerbated by the netting of her veil.

It wasn't until she and Grif were a third of the way down the aisle that she stopped dead in her carefully practiced, timed step. Her eyes filled with tears when she saw the two women seated in the front row. She probably had no idea that Tory was getting married, but there was something immensely touching about having her mother seated there to witness the wedding. Her nurse, Gladys, sat protectively beside her.

With a gentle nudge from Grif, Tory blinked back her tears and focused forward. If her mother's presence was a shock, seeing J.D., so magnificently gorgeous in his tuxedo, was a close second. His dark, sculpted features were contrasted by the crisp white shirt he wore and complemented by his rich black suit. A single pink rose was pinned to his lapel, a perfect match to the flowers she carried.

But it was more than just his appearance that held Tory enthralled. It was the look of sheer delight on his relaxed face as he watched her approach. There could have been ten thousand guests in the room for all she knew. Right then, at that moment, she saw no one but J.D.

Grif brought her to the appointed spot on the hearth and stood between Tory and her groom. Susan was at her side, stiff and grinning like a poorly snapped photograph.

The minister smiled at her and gave a small nod of his head, which immediately stopped the music. Tory listened as he spoke of the importance of the sanctity of marriage and all the attendant responsibilities of joining her life to J.D.'s. She was growing more nervous by the second.

"Who gives this woman to this man?" the minister asked.

"Her mother does," Grif answered. Apparently, he had known. He turned on his heels and left her to stand next to J.D.

After she relinquished her bouquet to Susan with visibly trembling hands, Tory turned and tilted her head back to meet his eyes. His expression was solemn.

The minister had them repeat their vows. Tory was glad when her "I do" came out in the same clear, assured fashion as his had just moments earlier.

"May I have the ring?" The minister directed the question to Wesley.

Tory's stomach dropped when Wesley produced a sparkling band of diamonds and sapphires. Her stomach positively lurched when J.D. slipped it onto her finger and it fit perfectly.

She heard the minister mumble something as J.D. reached for the edge of her veil and lifted it away from her tear-stained face. One of his arms went around her, pulling her against the solidness of his body. In the process, she was forced to arch her back to accommodate his superior height. She had known they would kiss—knew it was part of the ceremony. But it wasn't until she felt the first probing brush of his lips that Tory realized how very long she'd been waiting for this moment.

What began as a feather-light kiss exploded with all the flash and fury of a sudden summer squall. As the pressure of his mouth increased against hers, he pulled her more tightly into his arms.

Tory's head began to swim and she was certain J.D. could taste the burning embers of desire as his tongue moistened her lower lip.

And then it was over. Tory felt cheated, in spite of the rousing round of applause from the attendees when the minister pronounced them husband and wife.

Wife. That title was enough to jar her back to the present. As J.D. turned her to face the crowd, Tory was momentarily saddened to note the ever-blank expression on her mother's catatonic face. *I hope some part of her knows,* Tory appealed silently as Susan became the first of many well-wishers to hug Tory and offer congratulations.

While she was busy having her cheeks smeared with a rainbow of lipstick imprints, J.D. was receiving his share of best wishes. The organ music that had preceded the nuptials was replaced by the familiar sound of an Elvis ballad.

Josh shed his sports coat, moved behind the bar and began filling a neat row of glasses with champagne. The sounds of furniture scraping the floor was soon followed by the sound of Mickey the chef directing the serving staff through the throng of guests.

"It's nice to be served for a change," Susan whispered in her ear. "I'm still floored that Rose didn't tell me to run up and change out of my dress and get to work like she did Josh."

Tory smiled while her eyes scanned the crowded room for her husband. She found him deep in conversation with his brother.

"He sure is cute," Susan commented.

"J.D.?"

"You already know he's a hunk," Susan answered. "I was talking about the other one. The brother." She took a sip of champagne. "He's much better suited to me. His aura is a very cool, mellow green. I'm sensing serenity."

"I'm sensing nausea," Rose grumbled as she came up and wrapped her arm around Tory's waist. "The coed looks wonderful."

"Shelia?" Susan asked. "She's a really nice lady."

"If you happen to like husband-nabbing, children-stealing bleached blondes."

Tory smiled, knowing full well that Rose had her own roots attended to every third Thursday of the month.

"Oh...that's right," Susan said, the light dawning at its normally slow pace. "She's married to your ex. The guy standing over there with Grif."

"Maybe the mixture of Scotch and champagne will make Grif sick, and he'll barf all over Joe Don's tux," Rose said, a wicked gleam in her eyes.

"Not at Tory's wedding!" Susan wailed. "Really, Rose. It isn't good for your inner being to be so consumed with—"

"Shut up, Susan," Rose growled. "Go circulate and make sure all the guests have everything they need."

"But I'm not working," Susan pouted.

"We can change that," Rose told her, arching her eyebrow in a warning.

"Right," Susan said as she scurried into the crowd.

"Who are all these people?" Tory asked. "I recognize maybe a dozen, but where did you find the other eighty-eight?"

"Some are friends of mine, some are friends of Shelby's. Then I invited a few of the old gang who knew you when your dad owned the place."

"Speaking of which," Tory began, placing her hand on Rose's arm. Her newly acquired wedding band sparkled and sent out a series of prisms. "Thank you for making the arrangements for my mother to be here."

"Sorry to disappoint you, but I had nothing to do with that."

"Then who...?" Her voice trailed off as her eyes met J.D.'s. on the other side of the room.

"Your mother and that snotty nurse of hers are out on the side porch. You should run out and say your goodbyes now. J.D. could only manage to have her sprung for a few hours," Rose said.

Tory apologized her way through the maze of guests, her bouquet and gown gathered in her right hand for easy mobility.

"Gladys," she said as she stepped out into the mid-afternoon humidity. After they exchanged hugs, Tory carefully arranged her dress so that she could kneel in front of her mother.

"You look beautiful, Mama," she said, fingering the soft chiffon dress. "I'm so glad you were here to see this."

"I'm still trying to figure out what in the hell you're doing," Gladys said from behind the wheelchair.

Tory didn't meet the other woman's eyes. "I married a renowned architect."

"Who you haven't known long enough to make me believe this is some sort of love-at-first-sight thing. You seem to forget, child, *I've* known you a long time. This guy pays up your mother's back bills, and the very next week, I get instructions to bring her here for your wedding. So what gives?" Gladys demanded, her stern voice drowning out the din of conversation inside the Tattoo.

"Tory's a beautiful woman," she heard J.D. say as he appeared in the doorway. "Any man would be thrilled to have her as his wife."

She watched as Gladys sneered her disbelief at him. "She deserves better than just any man," she snapped at him.

J.D. smiled at the reprimand. "Then this was her lucky day," he said as his eyes moved to Tory. "The photographer needs us for a few minutes."

Before Tory could comment on the fact that no one had told her about any photographer or about any payments J.D. had made, the van from Ashley Villas pulled up to take Gladys and her mother home. Tory brushed a kiss on her mother's cheek and hugged Gladys.

"I'm still not buying it," Gladys whispered. "Something about all this just doesn't feel right."

"I know what I'm doing," Tory assured the caring woman. *I hope,* she added mentally as she watched her mother's frail body being lifted into the van.

"Thank you for arranging to have my mother here," Tory said shyly as she allowed J.D. to take her hand in his. The newly cut stones of the ring pressed into her flesh as she added, "And thank you for the ring. It really wasn't necessary."

It was the first time she could ever recall seeing J.D. look uncomfortable. "No big deal," was all he said as he quickened his pace.

"You found her!" Joseph Porter bellowed, his wife smiling at his side.

Rose was a few feet away, alternating between giving her ex-husband drop-dead looks and sneaking curious peeks at Shelia.

"Let's get this show on the road," the elder Mr. Porter yelled to the photographer and the other members of the wedding party.

"Between Rose and your father, I'm beginning to think you come by your dictatorial tendencies genetically," Tory whispered as she took her place in the center of the staged shot.

She smiled as she was blinded by several explosions from the flash above the camera. She lifted the flowers when instructed. She tilted her head, took a half-step closer to the groom, straightened her shoulders, handed Susan the bouquet, put the veil on, took the veil off. She did everything on command until the photographer said, "Give me a repeat of that kiss."

"I don't think—"

But J.D. somehow managed to silence her before she could even voice an objection. Wrapping her in the circle of his arms, he held her with one hand at her waist, the other at the base of her skull, slowly, inexorably, pulling her between his thighs. Her palms rested against the front of his jacket, and she found herself struggling to keep from balling the fabric into her fists when he teased her mouth open with his tongue. Deliberately and with incredible gentleness, J.D. seduced her with his kiss. If he would have raised his head and asked her to sneak back to his place, she would have—without hesitation.

Oddly enough, it was that very thought that convinced her to gently push him away. If he could make her feel this way with just a kiss, she was beginning to wonder what might happen when they were playing out their parts as husband and wife.

"Nicely done," she heard Wesley say.

Tory leaned against her husband, waiting for the strength to return to her legs. Without thinking, she touched a finger to her lips to feel the last remnants of the heat of his mouth.

"I always do my best," J.D. responded in a casual, conversational tone that managed to annoy Tory beyond reason. Her knees were like jelly and he was chatting as if he'd just patted his dog.

"*That* was your best?" she asked, making certain to inject a decent amount of disappointment in her tone. Flinging the end of her veil as if it were a mane of silky, long hair, Tory lifted her billowing skirt and decided to find herself a glass of champagne. She wanted to wash the taste of him from her mouth. And she wanted—no, needed—some space.

In a very unbridelike move, she grabbed a full glass off the bar and pushed her way into the kitchen, ignoring the startled stares of the staff. The only person she knew was Mickey, and he was too engrossed in some sort of puff pastry to notice her entrance.

She was followed into the kitchen, not by her groom, but by Detective Greer. She groaned into the glass before taking a long swallow.

"Nice wedding," he said over the clang of sheet pans being removed from the oven.

"Thanks," she responded flatly. The champagne had taken the edge off her annoyance, but Greer's sudden appearance threatened to send her back into a deep state of repressed frustration.

He moved in front of her, forcing her to meet his steady gaze. Tory blinked first, dropping her eyes to the small gold pin placed crookedly in the lapel of his drab gray jacket.

"You and the groom having your first fight?"

"Do you always interrogate brides at their weddings? Or am I getting special treatment?"

Greer shrugged. The action made his drugstore cologne more noticeable and more offensive. She took another sip of champagne. As she did so, Tory saw a shadowed face looking in through the portal-shaped window of the kitchen door. *Great,* she thought as she drained the glass. One of the guests was watching her being interrogated.

But when she turned to get a better look, the face was gone, leaving her to wonder if she might not have imagined it.

"He's having more pictures taken with his family."

"Who?" she asked.

"Your husband," Greer answered.

She could almost hear the thoughts rumbling through the detective's mind. Either he'd spoken with

Gladys, or he'd been trained well enough that he, too, had doubts about the motivation for the nuptials.

"Oh," was all she managed to say.

"I saw your mother here today."

Tory wished for another glass of champagne. Actually, she wished this day was over and behind her. "She's been taken home."

"Has she been that way ever since your father's murder?"

Tory gaped at him. "It's my wedding day, Detective. Must we discuss my father's murder and my mother's ill health?"

At least Greer had the courtesy to act chastened, but it was immediately apparent that her sarcasm would not deter him.

"Interesting guest list you put together," he remarked.

"I had nothing to do with it."

Greer obviously found her response of great importance. She could tell by the way his beady little eyes widened with blatantly rude curiosity.

"J.D. and his mother did the planning," she said, just to get this encounter over and done with. "If you want to know anything, I suggest you ask one of them."

"Most of the people that worked here at the time your father was murdered are out there in that room," he told her. "Considering how recently his body was discovered, I just wondered . . ."

"Sorry to disappoint you," she said. But she wasn't. "If you think we staged a wedding to bring all the suspects together in one room so that you could play Hercule Poirot, this isn't your day. The only hot things you'll find here today are cheese puffs and stuffed mushroom caps.''

Tory left him in a swirl of damask and netting. When she placed her hand on the door, she stared at her wedding band and felt the beginnings of guilt building in her stomach. It was a beautiful ring. And he'd made sure her mother had been there. The ceremony was lovely. She stood on tiptoe and glanced through the clouded window. It looked as if everyone was having a good time, and here she was pouting and hiding like a child. She never behaved like this, she thought as she took a deep breath. And she'd be damned if marrying J.D. Porter was going to change her in any way.

Chapter Twelve

"So, how was it?"

J.D. glared at his younger brother, knowing full well that Wes wasn't inquiring about the crystal-clear water or the lush greenery of the Bahamas. He was coiled so tightly that he was about to explode from spending seven days seeing his wife in the smallest bathing suit ever created and sleeping in the guest room of the cottage.

"After I drop you guys off, tell Tory that you and I have to run an errand so we can talk," Wesley said.

This time, J.D. heard urgency in his brother's voice. "Thanks all the same, Doc. But I don't need a private session with a shrink. After a whole week of look but don't touch, what I need is an agreeable woman."

He watched as Wes scanned the area near the ladies' room, which had swallowed his wife upon their arrival back in Charleston. Tory was just exiting, her frame shifted to accommodate the weight of the trinkets she had insisted on buying for every friend she had. J.D. felt his stomach knot and that all-too-familiar ache in his loins as he took in the sight of her shapely, tanned legs.

"It's important," Wes said emphatically. "Forget your libido for a while. I think you've got some serious trouble, brother."

"Such as?" J.D. asked, his curiosity running a distant second to his raging testosterone.

Tory joined them just as the luggage carousel whirred to life. "Such as what?" she asked.

J.D. felt his mouth drop open when he heard the relaxed tone of her voice. All week long, she'd spoken in nervous, high-pitched syllables, and then only when absolutely necessary. He might not have his brother's psychiatric credentials, but he knew then and there that he hadn't imagined the change down in the Bahamas.

"I was just asking J.D. if you could spare him for a little while this afternoon so that we could—"

"That's fine," Tory interrupted. "You guys do whatever."

Back at the condo, J.D. was still burned up by her almost grateful insistence that he go off with Wesley. In fact, she did everything but offer to walk their luggage the fifteen miles to his condo, strapped to her back.

What he couldn't figure out were the contradictions. She dressed conservatively, but had the sexiest lingerie of any woman he'd ever known. She had to know the effect she had on him. Hell, he'd spent most of his time lying on his stomach on the beach for fear his physical need for her would be obvious to the whole world. By the third day, he'd simply learned to wear shorts over his swimming trunks so as not to humiliate himself.

And he couldn't help wondering if she hadn't discovered his deception, and the little games were her way of punishing him. Asking him to put lotion on her, even moaning softly as his hands caressed her soft body. But that was the only time he'd been permitted to touch his wife. She'd made that clear on the first night.

He slammed out of the condo and left her sorting mail on the balcony. She'd offered to do all the unpacking, probably to get him out of there as soon as possible. "And Wes says I have trouble," he said to himself as he rode down in the elevator. *She must have found out.*

He muttered a rather colorful string of expletives as he stomped toward his car, where Wes was waiting.

"How did she find out?" J.D. demanded without preamble as he slid behind the wheel.

"What?"

"You said I had trouble. She found out, right?"

"Not that I'm aware of," Wes answered. "What I'm talking about is probably a hell of a lot worse than Tory discovering the real reason you married her."

"What could be worse than that?" J.D. asked sadly.

Wesley was genuinely surprised, judging from his shocked expression. "It sounds to me as if you might have developed some feelings for the lady."

"Most of which would get me arrested on a rape charge."

"J.D., pal, this is me, remember?" Wesley coaxed. "I can't believe it. You're in love with her, aren't you?"

"I want her," J.D. insisted, more to himself than his brother.

"Whatever," Wes said, reaching into the glove box of the car and removing a microrecorder. "We can talk about your denial at some later date. You've got to listen to this.''

''What is it?''

''Just listen!'' Wes grumbled insistently as he pressed a button on the machine.

There was the recognizable tone of an answering-machine tape, then a muffled, almost indecipherable voice began to speak.

''I saw you with that cop at your wedding.'' The voice paused for a throaty chuckle. ''You didn't know I was there, did you? You made a pretty bride, but a stupid one. I was close enough to count the pearls on your dress, did you know that?''

There was another pause, almost long enough to give J.D. the impression that the cryptic message was ended. He was wrong.

''Your mother doesn't look well. But she's doing better than your father, isn't she? If you keep lighting fires under that detective, something bad will happen. I'll give you one last chance to show me you can be a good girl. Don't disappoint me, now. And just so you know I'm capable of dealing you the same fate I dealt your father, I'll be sending you a little token.''

Chapter Thirteen

He could hear her scream all the way down in the parking lot. J.D. wasted no time in abandoning his car and making a dash back toward the building. The sound of his brother's racing footsteps echoed along with his own.

"Come on! Come on!" J.D. urged as his finger jabbed impatiently at the button to summon the elevator.

It seemed to take forever before he and Wes were finally making the ascent to the top floor. When he burst into the apartment, he wasn't sure what shocked him the most—the fact that Tory flung herself into his arms, or that she had a gun.

"I'll take this," he heard Wes say behind him.

J.D. then felt her hold on him tighten. He could also feel the rapid beat of her heart as her small form shook and shivered in his arms.

Stroking her hair, he whispered soothing words, trying to comprehend this surprise. His eyes scanned the room, then he spotted the torn, decorative wedding paper and open shoe box on the dining room table.

Apparently, his brother had seen the same thing, because as J.D. stood comforting his shaken wife, Wes went to examine the gift. A rusty pistol dangled from between his thumb and forefinger.

"I take it this *thing* was sent to you here?" Wes asked.

Tory nodded, her face buried against J.D.'s chest. Wetness from her silent tears dampened the fabric of his shirt with her jerky movements.

Tory sucked in a deep breath and, as if she just then realized that she had automatically gone to him for support, she jumped back. Wiping the remains of her tears with the back of her hand, he watched her force an apologetic smile to her still-trembling lips. He also noticed she wouldn't meet his eyes.

She went to Wes, obviously more interested in explaining the situation to him, J.D. thought. The realization made him feel oddly jealous of his younger brother. While his intellect told him that it made perfect sense for an upset woman to seek out a psychiatrist, the emotional side of him resented her choice.

"I was stacking up the gifts that were delivered while we were away and when I got to this one..." Her voice trailed off and she wrapped her arms around herself, still visibly upset.

"Is there a return address?" J.D. asked.

Using a pen and great care, he flipped the paper over and found nothing.

"That's why I opened it," Tory said. "There was no card, so I was hoping I'd find one inside so we'd know who to thank."

"And instead, you got that," J.D. concluded, taking the weapon from his brother for a closer look.

Along with the rust, he could easily see small grains of sandy soil embedded in the barrel and in the spaces between the butt and the trigger. "Good God," he muttered softly.

"What?" Wes asked.

"I'm no expert, but this is the same kind of soil we've been excavating around the dependency to shore up the foundation."

His eyes met and held Tory's. The sight of unshed tears and damp lashes caused an instant, almost reflexive, anger to singe each and every cell in his body. "We've got to call Greer."

"No," she insisted with a fervent shake of her head. As if the box had contained an ugly set of pot holders, Tory added, "Let's just throw it in the trash and forget it."

"We have to turn it over to the cops," he said in a firm but soft tone. His instant refusal of her plan brought more tears to her eyes. Placing one hand on her shoulder and the other at her chin, he gently forced her face up. "You can't just toss something like a gun in the trash. No telling who might wind up with it."

"He's right," Wes chimed in. "You can't take a risk like that. You have an obligation to turn it over to the police."

Tory shrugged away from him and moved out onto the balcony. J.D. looked to his brother for guidance.

"I'm guessing this was what her mysterious caller referred to when he said he'd send her a little token," Wes surmised.

"I've got to tell her I know about the call, and..." he paused and felt a helplessness he hadn't known for years. "I've got to know how long this has been going on."

J.D. opened and closed his fists. He began to pace, his thoughts racing furiously through his mind.

"You know," Wes said, "until the police have a look at this, you have no way of knowing whether it has any connection to her father's murder."

"If I tell her that, it might calm her down," J.D. said, feeling somewhat more in control. "God knows, there are enough kooks out there that this gun and the call could be nothing more than the acts of a—"

"Mentally unstable individual," Wes concluded.

"I prefer kook," J.D. retorted rather hotly. "I doubt you'd be feeling very charitable if it was your wife being harassed. I also doubt you'd give a flying hoot about the guy's mental stability."

"Your *wife?*" Wes asked in that calm-shrink voice. "Very possessive language from a man who claims he only married her to—"

"Can it!"

He could tell by the expression on his brother's face that he wanted to pursue this area further, but J.D. wasn't about to risk Tory's overhearing anything incriminating. Especially if she had already discovered his deception.

"Take one of those straw bags Tory bought in the islands and put all this stuff in there," J.D. instructed. "And try not to get your fingerprints all over it."

"Why me?" Wes queried.

J.D. rolled his eyes. "Whoever sent this knew her home phone number, when and who she married and my address. You can't just go traipsing out of the building with that damned gun under your arm. For all we know, he could be watching this place."

"Or she."

J.D. gave his brother a questioning look. "A woman?"

"Could you determine gender from that tape?" Wes asked. "I couldn't."

"Then take the tape and the gun to Greer and let the police sort it all out. Just make sure no one sees you contact the cops." He glanced out to Tory's motionless body, her ramrod-stiff back to him. "I'll see what I can find out from her."

"Word to the wise?" Wes asked as he carefully filled one of the straw bags.

"As long as it's only one word."

"Two."

"Fine."

"Tread lightly."

"Lord, Wesley," J.D. growled softly. "Give me a little credit for knowing better than to bulldoze the lady."

"You've been known to bulldoze more than just construction sights in the past," Wes told him with a pointed look. "I'm just telling you that Tory is in a very fragile emotional state right now. You could do some real damage to her if you start interrogating her about something as painful as the murder of her father."

"Thank you," J.D. said, sarcasm in each syllable. "Don't forget to bill me for your services."

Wes was obviously hurt by the dig. "I'm only warning you that she's exhibiting all the classic symptoms of a person running out of coping mechanisms. Push hard enough, and you might just destroy her."

"I know," J.D. said as he gave his brother's shoulder an apologetic squeeze. "Her mother's a vegetable. It hasn't been that long since we found her father. Now, some loony is after her."

"And don't forget yourself, J.D. If she doesn't already know your real reasons for marrying her, I'd advise against your sharing that bit of information for the moment. Wait until some of these other issues are resolved first." Wes slung the bag over his shoulder and went for the door. He stopped and turned back to add, "Who knows? The reason you asked her to marry you may be moot. *If* your behavior is any indication of what's going on inside your head."

"Stay out of my head," J.D. retorted. "I'll decide how to deal with Tory all by myself."

"You're doing a great job so far," Wes remarked as he slipped from the condo.

J.D. JOINED HER on the balcony just as humidity began to paint the sky an oppressive gray. "Looks like a storm's coming," she said, then smiled wryly at the inadvertent metaphor. "I'm sorry I overreacted like that." She looked up into his expressionless face. "If you're afraid you'll spend the next few months married to a screamer, I can assure you, it was just the shock."

With her fingernail, she traced the carved pattern on the newel post at the edge of the railing. Thanks to their trip to the islands, her skin was the same dark, rich color as the wood. Also thanks to their honeymoon, tension connected them more than the vows they had exchanged just a week earlier.

One look into the shimmering emotion in his eyes told her all she needed to know. He still wasn't over her proclamation that they would never share a bed. Not that she wasn't tempted. *Was she ever!* Even when she'd been distraught over the gun, she'd been aware of him on that primal level. Her body still begged for the comfort she felt in his arms, for the excitement she felt whenever she caught the scent of his cologne.

But there was something else in those gray depths that she hadn't seen before. Something she couldn't easily define.

"I should have picked up on it before now, but—"

"Wait!" she interrupted, swallowing the sudden rush of embarrassment that was quickly filling her body. "It isn't your fault," she said, dropping her eyes to stare at the tips of his slightly scuffed loafers. "I should have told you about it before we got married. I guess I just thought it wouldn't matter since this isn't a real marriage and I—"

"It's real enough so that you shouldn't have hidden something this important from me until now."

Tory's embarrassment very quickly turned to indignation. "This is in name only," she reminded him. "That was the deal we made in my apartment, so stop trying to make me feel guilty for not telling you something so intimate about myself. I didn't owe you any explanations then, and I'm not about to give you any now."

She took less than two steps before J.D.'s arm caught hers, halting her rather dramatic exit from the balcony. With a less than subtle yank, he had her trapped against him. She knew if she insisted, J.D. would let her go in an instant. She didn't know why she didn't insist.

"Back up," he said, his forehead wrinkled in a questioning frown. "What makes you think your little secret was none of my business? It became my business the instant you agreed to marry me."

"In name only," she reminded him through gritted teeth.

"And your name is now Victoria Porter," he told her pointedly and with sufficient arrogance to make her feel like a possession rather than a person.

"Big deal," she taunted with a particularly snotty little smile for effect. "That still doesn't mean I have to bare my soul to you. Especially since my name will go right back to Conway the minute I have my degree."

Watching his eyes was like watching the sky. They grew more and more threatening with each passing second.

"I'm sorry," she said when she could no longer stand the silent contempt emanating from his large form. "I know you're the one doing me a favor, so I should be grateful to you for—"

"I don't want your damned gratitude," he shouted back at her. "I want to know why you didn't say something about this to me before now."

Tory placed her palms against his chest. She heard the sharp intake of his breath. Her touch seemed to have that effect on him each and every time she grew bold enough to try it. "I guess I assumed that our marriage was more like a business deal, and so I didn't think it was important."

"Not important?" he scoffed.

"So now that you know," she said, her fingers tentatively toying with the hard muscle beneath his shirt, "you can stop being angry with me."

He gaped at her and she felt the corded strength beneath her palms flinch at her remark.

"If anything, I'm more angry that you didn't bother to tell me from the start."

Exasperated, Tory flattened her hands and pushed away from him, though their eyes remained locked in some level of silent combat.

"And when, oh exalted one, was I supposed to broach this subject with you?"

"Instantly," he responded as he shifted his weight to a menacing, legs-braced-shoulder's-width-apart stance.

She chuckled. "Sorry, your lordship, but I don't make a habit of introducing myself as Victoria Conway, oldest living virgin in the state of South Carolina."

J.D. blinked, and apparently it had nothing to do with the first crashing boom of thunder. At that moment, the heavens opened up, spitting quarter-size drops of rain, which quickly evolved into a single sheet of water.

Tory made it inside first, amazed by how wet she had gotten in the few seconds it took to open the sliding glass door. The air-conditioning cooled her damp skin to the point of producing goose bumps.

Two things struck her as she took in her surroundings. First, the gun and all its trimmings were gone. The second thing was that, amazingly, J.D. went directly to the sofa and was just sitting there. His expression made her shiver. It was too close to the look her mother had worn for the past fifteen years.

"You already figured it out," she began to argue. "So why are you sitting there like that?"

"Virgin?" he said, swallowing as if the word left an unpleasant taste in his mouth.

"It *is* fashionable these days," she defended. "Or haven't you realized that the previous generation had free love, Woodstock and LSD, while my generation has AIDS, gangbangers and crack?''

"You're a virgin," he mumbled.

"Will you stop saying that word like I'm some sort of leper?" she said with a moan. "And why am I bothering to explain my personal choices to you, when you obviously ignored my wishes regarding the gun?"

Mention of the weapon seemed to bring him out of his stupor. Tory wasn't really sure whether that was good or bad.

"Wes is taking it to Greer."

Closing her eyes, Tory rubbed her forehead and in a small, frightened voice asked, "Do you have any idea how much trouble you might have caused me by doing that?"

"That's what I was talking about out on the balcony."

"The gun?"

"The trouble," he corrected with a wry smile. "Though your little bombshell fits into that category also, as far as I'm concerned."

Tory glared at him. "You mean you didn't know why I made you sleep in the guest room of the cottage when we were in the Bahamas?"

"I thought it was your way of putting me off until we knew each other better."

Tory didn't know whether to laugh at the absurdity of his testosterone-driven reasoning, or slap him for his arrogant certainty that she'd fall into bed with him. "Here's an update for you," she said with a saccharine smile. "I don't sleep with men just because I know them well. So you can forget that idea."

"Fine with me," he returned in the same tone. "I'm not much into virgin sacrifice, myself."

"Then it's settled."

"Fine."

"Fine," she agreed as she moved over to open her suitcase. "I'm going to take my mother the necklace I bought her in Paradise Island."

"I don't think that's a smart move."

"Frankly, J.D., right about now, I really don't give two damns what you think."

"MAKING UP THE SOFA," Wes said without attempting to keep a smug grin off his face. "You must have done a great job handling the missus."

"Shut up," J.D. told his brother.

"Speaking of Tory, where is she?"

"She went to see her mother."

Wes nodded as concern crept into his expression. "How long ago?"

"Late afternoon," J.D. said as he punched a pillow into place.

"Do you realize it's almost ten o'clock?" Wesley asked.

"Of course I do. I learned to tell time before you did."

Wes sighed. "Have you heard from her?"

"Nope."

"That isn't very smart, given the fact that some unbalanced individual seems to have a fixation where she's concerned."

"I've been calling Ashley Villas every half hour. She's sitting with her mother, and they'll have security walk her to her car when she decides to come home."

Sitting on his "bed," J.D. frowned at the contemplative stare he was getting from his brother. "What did you expect me to do?'' he thundered. "Tell her she couldn't go? *You* try telling Tory she can't do something. See how far you get.''

"I'm sensing hostility, J.D.''

"Any more of your psycho-babble and you'll be sensing my fist.''

"I'm not trying to probe.''

"Nonsense,'' J.D. retorted with a snort. "You want to know what happened after you left?'' It was a rhetorical question and Wes remained silent but attentive. "We argued, then she left to see her mother.''

"Avoidance is how some people deal with confrontation. When the fire gets hot, they simply run from the flames instead of trying to quell the embers.''

"I don't know why you're thinking of opening a practice in Miami,'' J.D. commented glibly. "Seems to me you have enough work right here to keep you busy for the next decade or so.''

"It doesn't surprise me that she sought solace with her mother. Pretty predictable behavior. Her mother's very safe. It's not like that woman will ask her questions or make any comments.'' Wes took the seat directly across from him as he pushed the frame of his glasses higher on the bridge of his nose. "You must not have been very calm when you explained the rationality of turning the gun over to the police, or she wouldn't have gone running to her catatonic mother.''

"We barely discussed the gun.''

Wes's dark eyebrows arched high above the rim of his glasses. "So you must have blurted out that we listened to the tape from her answering machine, which I gave to Greer.''

"You did what?''

The sound of Tory's horrified and angry words filled the room.

"J.D. asked me to monitor the movers," Wes explained.

"Your caller left another threatening message for you," J.D. said without preamble or the guidance of his younger brother's warning look. "That's why you had the phone off the hook before we got married, right?"

"I can't believe you had the audacity to invade my privacy. How dare you listen to my private telephone messages and then send your brother off to the police with my tape without so much as discussing it with me."

"Really?" J.D. got to his feet with lightning speed. "You're my wife."

"Children," Wes interrupted, rising so that he stood directly between them. "I think you're both overreacting just a bit."

Wes turned toward Tory and said, "We only turned over the tape to the police because of its threatening nature and our concern for your welfare."

Then he turned back to J.D., his face far more reasonable than Tory's sour expression, and said, "A wife is no longer chattel, J.D., so I suggest you think of a better explanation when you do something stupid where Tory is concerned."

J.D. watched as Tory bit her bottom lip to keep from giggling as she listened to the excellent tongue-lashing that went on for several more minutes. Once Wes was finished, J.D. felt like a chastised pupil who'd just been taken down a notch by the teacher.

Reluctantly, he peered around his brother and met her eyes. "I'm sorry."

"No problem," she answered.

The simple act of apologizing seemed to drain every ounce of hostility from her. It was amazing, he thought, that she could be so accepting, especially considering some of the truly ignorant things he'd said.

"I hate to interrupt meaningful communication between spouses, but I need to tell you what happened when I saw Greer." Wesley guided Tory over to J.D. before continuing. "The initial ballistics report confirms that the gun you received as a wedding present was, in fact, the gun that killed your father."

Chapter Fourteen

Tory swayed, but managed to remain standing on her own two feet, aided by J.D.'s hand bracing her waist. "How can they know that?" she asked.

Wesley shrugged uncomfortably. "They fire the gun into some sort of barrel and then compare the bullet to the one they recovered from the scene."

"Are they checking it for prints?" she heard J.D. ask.

"It'll take a day or two before the police lab does everything they need to do on the gun, the shoe box and the wrapping paper," Wes explained. "Oh," he cleared his throat nervously and added, "you both have to go down and be printed. They printed me, Dad and Shelia."

"For what?" Tory asked, incredulous at the mere thought of being fingerprinted.

"We all touched the stuff. They need to rule out our fingerprints."

"We'll go down first thing in the morning," J.D. assured his brother. "Why this sudden change of plans?" J.D. asked his brother.

Wes shrugged before walking wordlessly out the door of the condo.

THE NEXT MORNING, on their way back from the police station, they were separated by the smooth leather console of the Mercedes, as well as by the silence that had begun when they had said good-night the previous evening. Unlike his playful attempts and teasing pressures in the Bahamas, J.D. had barely spoken to her since he had staked out his territory on the sofa.

She'd argued with him about that. A brief exchange on the absurdity of her sleeping in that huge bed, while he was cramped on the small sofa. But he'd been adamant, and she was fully aware of the fact that once J.D. made up his mind about something, it was pointless to try to sway him.

If the redness around the gray in his eyes was any indication, he hadn't slept well. Neither had she, but her restlessness had had nothing to do with the accommodations. His scent clung to the pillows and small reminders of him were everywhere in that bedroom. And, she thought glibly, she had been listening for him through the wall. She was aware of his tossing and turning, his muffled curses and the fact that he'd gone into the kitchen three times during the night.

"Sleep well?" he asked.

"Your bed is very comfortable," she hedged. "And large enough to be a football field."

His chuckle was deep and throaty—it relaxed much of the tension twisting her insides. "I guess it must have felt that way to you. That thing you had in your apartment wasn't much bigger than an army-issue cot."

"It was," she said. "Actually, it was navy issue. I got it at one of those secondhand places near the naval base."

She watched his profile as he shook his head. He steered the ultraexpensive car with just the thumb and forefinger of his right hand. In spite of his apparent tiredness, J.D. still looked incredibly handsome in his jeans and black polo shirt. Noting the crisp folds on his shirtsleeves, it suddenly dawned on her that he had his clothing professionally cleaned and pressed. She stifled a grin when she had the silly thought that he probably had his underwear dry-cleaned, as well.

"Do you have enough room in the closets and the dressers?"

"Plenty," she said, wondering if he had somehow read her mind. "I'm not much of a clothes freak."

A frown curled the corners of his mouth downward. "I've noticed."

"That's just a tad unkind," she told him, lowering her eyes to stare at the remnants of ink imbedded in the pads of her fingers.

"I wasn't trying to be unkind," he said softly, taking his eyes off the road for just an instant. "I just like seeing you in your girl clothes."

Tory looked at her outfit and felt very much like Cinderella long before the fairy godmother showed up.

"You wear dresses that remind me of my grandmother's nightgown," he explained without malice in his soft tone. "You're always covered from your throat to your ankles."

"Gee, thanks."

"You're a very pretty woman, Tory. There's no need for you to camouflage yourself. Especially now."

"Why not now?"

"Because you have a wedding ring on your finger and a husband that will pound anyone who says anything about your..." He began to stammer.

"Top heaviness?" she finished defensively.

She saw his sexy half smile before he said, "Voluptuousness."

Somehow, the single word managed to ignite those all-too-familiar fires in the pit of her stomach.

"You have a credit card. Use it."

"I did," she returned. "I'm surprised it didn't warp from all those machines it went through in the Bahamas."

"I'm not talking about using it for gifts for other people. I want you to get some things for yourself. Whatever you want."

"I don't need new things," she insisted.

"I'm not suggesting you buy clothing as sexy as your undergarments, but, Tory, there is such a thing as middle ground."

He noticed her bras and panties? "I suppose I could be persuaded to buy just a few things."

"Persuaded?"

"If you agree to have Rose over for dinner tomorrow night, I'll agree to go shopping."

"Fine," he said quickly. Too quickly.

"And you have to be civil and treat her with kindness. Maybe you could even call her Mom—just once."

She could almost feel the tension grip his body as tightly as he now gripped the wheel.

"You don't understand the situation," he growled.

"Really?" Tory turned in her seat and spoke directly to the hard set of his jaw. "Until a month ago, I thought my father had abandoned me and I hated him for it. Obviously, I'm very sad to know he's been dead all these years. But understanding the reason he wasn't a part of my life has lifted an incredible weight from my shoulders."

"That's you."

"And you," she said as she placed a tentative hand on his forearm. "I know what it feels like to deal with the hurt of thinking one of your parents didn't love you enough to make you a part of their life. I also know the anger and the guilt that comes with those emotions. I still deal with those feelings every time I visit my mother."

She saw his expression soften just a fraction.

"For the first five years she was in the hospital, I visited out of a sense of duty. I never talked to her or asked her doctors about her condition. I just stared at her, hoping, on the one hand, that she would see my contempt, and terrified, on the other hand, of the very same thing."

"You and Wes apparently took the same Psych 101 course."

"The difference between your situation and mine," she said, ignoring his gibe, "is that *you* have the ability to build some sort of relationship with your mother. I don't. If you continue to treat her to punishing looks and forced cordiality, you might just achieve your apparent goal of keeping her out of your life."

"I'll take your advice under consideration," he said as they turned into the alleyway beside the Rose Tattoo. "Right now, though, we've got some work to do."

It was frustrating to realize that her husband was so close-minded about Rose. Tory suspected that with Shelia in town, the problem would only get worse. His warmth toward his stepmother would have been obvious to the blind. And it wasn't lost on Rose.

Tory and J.D. entered the restaurant through the kitchen door. It was quiet, though the reprieve was temporary. Mickey would be there any moment to begin prepping for the lunch crowd. Tory felt very strange out of uniform.

But that wasn't as strange as what they discovered in the dining room. Instead of doing setups, Susan was seated at one of the round tables near the horseshoe-shaped bar, holding Wes's hand, her attention riveted to his open palm resting in hers.

"This ought to be rich," J.D. whispered against her ear.

That simple action caused a tingling to dance along her spine to where his fingers splayed at her waist.

"...hiding something," Susan was saying. "You're definitely struggling with this deception. I see it in your aura as well as your palm, so I know this is a definite problem in your life."

Tory felt his hand fall away from her and stifled the urge to pull it back into place. She wandered over to her brother-in-law and Susan, while J.D. went to the mantel and overmantel and began to study the intricate, decorative woodwork of both.

"It's almost ten o'clock," Tory told her friend. "If Rose comes down and sees you playing soothsayer, she'll ream you but good."

Susan pouted and sighed. "The new girl—her name's Becky—was supposed to be here ten minutes ago. Once she arrives, we can do the setups in a flash."

"Hello," Wes offered, a mischievous look in his eyes. "Greer called here not ten minutes ago looking for you and J.D."

"We've already been to the station and been printed." She held out her stained fingers for his inspection.

"It wasn't about the prints," Wes said as his expression grew somber. "I think you should return his call."

Tory turned toward the bar, but Wes called her back.

"It would probably be better if J.D. called."

"Called who?" J.D. asked.

J.D. came and stood at her side. She knew he was only playing the attentive-husband role for Susan. Yet Wes looked very interested when J.D.'s large hand found hers.

"Greer. I left the number on a napkin next to the phone."

J.D. let out a colorful expletive, then took her along with him as he went to the bar to make the call.

"I see," he said into the receiver.

"See what?" Tory mouthed. J.D. ignored her, but did give her hand a gentle squeeze.

"So it's a dead end. What about the tape?" J.D.'s expression grew dark and impatient. "Well, how long will that take?"

There were a few more short, clipped questions before J.D. ended the call on a less than polite note.

Spinning one of the bar stools, he pulled her into the V created by his opened thighs. Tory would have preferred a slightly less intimate position, but she was too curious about the developments with the police, not to mention the feel of being held by his powerful legs.

"They traced the gun."

"And?"

"It was registered to your father."

"I never knew Daddy had a gun," she blurted out.

"That tells me something."

"Really? What?"

"That if you didn't know he had a weapon, he didn't keep it out in plain sight. That limits the number of people who knew he had a gun."

Tory nodded at his deduction. "Or he could have bragged about it the way Evan bragged about all those poor dead animals mounted in his office."

"We'll check that out. What about your friend Grif?" J.D. suggested. "If your father made the gun common knowledge, wouldn't Grif be able to tell us that?"

"Definitely," Tory said. "And he'll tell me the truth."

"Unless he's the one that pulled the trigger," J.D. said.

Tory took a step back, annoyed that he would even suggest such a thing. "That man walked me down the aisle, for heaven's sake! Do you think he would have done something like that if he had killed my father?" Before J.D. could respond, she continued, "Even before I came to work here, Grif used to come and visit me at my grandmother's. He can't possibly be involved in my father's murder."

"Just like he doesn't go fishing with Evan?"

That silenced her. The memory of that photograph in Evan's office had bothered her from the first instant she'd laid eyes on it. She couldn't ever remember Grif saying anything about a fishing buddy. Tory had always assumed he went off on his own.

"Or have private conversations with some well-dressed guy in his early fifties out on the porch," J.D. added. "I recognized him, I just can't place him."

"What are you talking about?"

"At our wedding, when I went looking for you when the photographer needed us, I saw Grif out on the front porch with this guy. I couldn't hear what was being said, but I can assure you they weren't discussing the good old days."

"So that makes Grif a suspicious character?" she defended. "For all you know, he could have just been telling this mysterious man that the restaurant was closed for the day."

J.D. looked as if he wanted to argue, but the sudden arrival of a flustered brunette forced him to let her have the last word on the subject. Tory smiled, knowing it might be the one and only time she'd ever get the last word in an argument with her husband.

Husband? that little voice inside her head questioned. She couldn't afford to start thinking of J.D. as anything more than the means to an end. She had married him to become eligible for a grant, something she seemed to keep forgetting.

"I'm so sorry I'm late," the woman gushed to J.D. "I'm not really used to the city and I got lost."

"Becky, I take it?" J.D. asked, offering the woman a warm smile.

It was warm enough so that Tory got to watch the woman melt right before her eyes. She wasn't real thrilled by the new employee's reaction to J.D.—nor her own reaction, which she silently acknowledged was jealousy.

"Rose is upstairs," Tory told her, annoyed that she had to look up to the taller woman. "I suggest you check in with her."

"Rose?" the brunette repeated, noticing Tory for the first time.

"The owner?" Tory supplied. "This is the Rose Tattoo, surely you can grasp the connection."

The woman colored and followed Susan back through the kitchen.

"Ouch," J.D. said.

"What?"

"That was just a little on the catty side, wouldn't you say?"

"She's supposed to be here to work, not ogle your body."

The poorly hidden grin on his face widened and evolved into a purely satisfied smile. "She wasn't ogling my body. But now that we're on the subject, hers wasn't too bad," he added, stroking the faint growth of stubble on his chin.

"If you happen to like women who look like they've thrown up everything they've ever eaten. She was as thin as a rail," Tory said. "She's probably got one of those eating disorders."

"Oh, I don't know," he said. "She was a tad on the lean side, but I think you're going a little overboard."

Overboard this, Tory thought as she turned away from J.D., hiding a rather unladylike display of her tongue from one and all.

Wes, who sat nursing a watered-down soda, looked up as she approached him at the table. She could hear J.D. on the phone as she joined her brother-in-law.

Unlike J.D., Wes always appeared calm and amiable. Through the lenses of his glasses, she could see no trace of the volatility that changed J.D.'s eyes from a soft gray to a stormy silver.

"I can't believe you were letting Susan do a reading," she said. "I would think, as a psychiatrist, you wouldn't put much stock in all that metaphysical garbage.''

Wes shrugged. ''To a lot of people, it isn't garbage—hence, the proliferation of psychic hotlines.''

''Point.'' Tory laughed. ''Did it bother you when her 'sight' came so close to the truth?''

''I don't understand your question.''

Tilting her head to one side, Tory gave him a sidelong glance. ''C'mon, Wes. I *know* that you know about J.D. and me.''

Wes didn't so much as flinch. ''I know that unconventional circumstances brought you together.''

''J.D. is right.''

Wes adjusted his glasses. ''About what?''

''That you can't turn off the psychiatrist in you, even for your own family.''

Wes smiled. ''And...'' The pause was pointed and deliberate. ''You are part of my family now, aren't you?''

''Just passing through,'' she assured him. ''But I appreciate all your kindness. If I had a sibling who did something as stupid as marry a woman just so she could finish grad school, I'm not sure I could be quite so accepting.''

''J.D.'s reasons for marrying you are his own business. I don't stand in judgment of anyone.''

''Or tell your own father the truth?''

Raising his arms, Wes said, ''That's J.D.'s call.''

''But you advised him against it?''

''Yes.''

Tory felt a sudden chill in the air that had nothing to do with the gentle breeze of the paddles of the whirling fans overhead. She'd asked for it. What had she been hoping for? That J.D. had confided in his brother that he had some genuine feelings for her?

Tory turned to watch J.D. Why was she suddenly questioning his motives? It wasn't as if *she* had any feelings for him. Then why do you feel safe and content when he's around? that annoying little voice in her head asked.

"What about you?" Wes asked.

"What about me?"

"I was just wondering about your feelings about all this."

Tory frowned at him. "Shall I lie on a couch to answer that?"

Wes chuckled. "I'm just curious. Which is probably why I became a psychiatrist. People fascinate me."

And J.D. fascinates me, her brain answered without hesitation. "Then hang around here. There's lots of work to be done."

Arching back in his chair, Wes met her gaze. "Funny. That's exactly what J.D. said to me."

"Wes," she began in an almost pleading tone, "I need a friend, not an analysis. I'd like your friendship, but I've bccn dealing with my mother's psychiatrists for years, and I'm not interested in anyone delving into my psyche."

"How are you at delving into finding me someone who can replicate those?" J.D. asked as he came up behind her, pointing at the decorative pieces on the upper mantel of the fireplace. The fireplace in the dependency was crude, almost primitive. A decision had been made to re-create the flavor of the Tattoo in the dependency.

"I know the perfect person," Tory said. "He's got a shop over on Market. If we cast one of the originals, he can duplicate it down to the most minute detail."

"Then we'll use him for the fireplace. I've got a guy in Miami who'll fabricate new door handles and some of the other iron pieces."

The chair scraped against the floor as she looked up at him quizzically. "You haven't even finished shoring up the foundation. What's the hurry for the detail stuff?"

"I do have other clients, Tory," he answered, his expression unreadable. "If the pieces sit on the floor until it's time to—"

J.D. was silenced by the loud, fast entrance of Chad Tanner. The toddler came barreling up to the table at full throttle. Had it not been for J.D.'s quick reaction, Chad probably would have knocked himself unconscious on contact.

"Slow down, tiger," he told the startled little boy.

Shelby, looking positively wilted from the heat, waddled in from the kitchen. She didn't look very happy.

"I told you to wait for me," she said to her son. "One of these days, you're going to get hurt."

Unbeknownst to Shelby, J.D. was making silly faces at the little boy, which had the predictable effect. Chad began to laugh.

"It's not funny," Shelby continued.

"J.D.'s the real culprit here," Tory explained.

The big man tossed the child high in the air several times, until the little boy was positively squealing with delight and begging for more.

Chad's dark coloring made her wonder what a son of J.D.'s might look like. Probably similar to the child he appeared happy to entertain.

"You and Dylan," Shelby grumbled as she motioned J.D. to put Chad down. "It's no wonder this child is such a terror. Dylan plays with him when the child is supposed to be napping. Now you're making him laugh when he should be feeling repentant for disobeying."

Taking her son by the hand, Shelby moved back toward the kitchen. "This baby," she said, referring to the bulge of her abdomen, "will not be as spoiled as her older brother."

"I doubt it," Tory said under her breath when Shelby was out of earshot. "Chad was kidnapped a few months ago. The guy that took him really tormented Shelby and Dylan before they got the little guy back. They were so glad to have him home that I don't think either Dylan or Shelby will properly discipline that boy."

"I'd take a spoiled child over a missing one any day," J.D. said. "Keep Wes company while I go and talk to Rose. When I'm finished, we'll go see your friend about the cornices."

"Okay," Tory managed to say, slightly hurt by what she perceived as his desire to put some distance between them. Her emotions were salved when he returned in under five minutes with his keys dangling from one square-tipped finger.

AFTER THEY HAD arranged for the delicate replication work to be done, J.D. surprised her by asking if they could drop in on Grif.

"Under what pretext?"

"That poster of tropical fish you bought for him in the Bahamas is in the trunk. I thought you might want to drop off the gift."

"And I think you have an ulterior motive."

"Me?" he repeated, feigning shock. "Okay, so I wouldn't mind an explanation of who he was fighting with at the wedding. And if he knew about your father's gun."

Tory slid her lower lip between her teeth as she contemplated the possible ramifications of interrogating a friend. She was also wary that the mysterious caller might get wind of it. *I'm being silly,* she told herself. The caller could only find out if Grif was somehow connected to the murder.

She directed J.D. to a small, waterfront home in Folly Beach. Time and tide had toyed with the pilings, so the house now leaned conspicuously toward the surf.

"Apparently, Grif isn't doing as well as his buddy Evan," J.D. observed as they climbed the wooden steps meant to keep the house safely above flood level.

Grif seemed very surprised when he opened the door and found the two of them on his doorstep. J.D. filed that little tidbit in the back of his mind.

The white-haired man hugged Tory and glowered at him. J.D. didn't much care if the old man liked him, he was more intent on making sure Tory wasn't placing her trust in a potentially dangerous man.

Grif tossed aside a wad of newspaper and offered them drinks. Tory declined, he asked for a beer. When Grif went into the kitchen, J.D. moved over to study some of the various photographs crudely framed on one wall. He found a duplicate of the one in Evan's office, but it wasn't nearly as interesting as the one he spotted below it.

"Here's your beer," Grif said, tapping the bottle against J.D.'s shoulder.

"I see you've been fishing for quite a number of years," J.D. commented.

"Since I was big enough to hold a rod."

"You also seem to have lots of different partners."

J.D. turned so that he could watch the older man's expression. He read caution in his eyes and anger in the deep lines next to Grif's sun-blistered lips.

"I'm always up for fishing. Don't much care who asks."

"Tory," J.D. said without actually looking at his wife, "we forgot to get Grif's present out of the trunk." He tossed her the keys. "Why don't you go and get it since you were the one that picked it out."

She did, not because he'd issued an order, he noted, but because he could tell that the tension building between Grif and himself was making her uncomfortable.

"She thinks the world of you," J.D. said offhandedly as he took a swallow of the bitter beer.

"You got a problem with that?" Grif asked, his tone defensive.

"Only if you know something about her father's murder."

"Bob Conway was my friend," Grif stated. "If I'd have known he was murdered, I would have gone to the authorities immediately."

"Did you know about the gun?"

Grif's forehead wrinkled at the question. "What gun?"

"The one Bob Conway owned."

Grif scratch his unshaven chin. "I think he kept a pistol behind the bar, but I couldn't swear to it. Why?"

"The man was shot. I was just wondering."

"Listen," Grif began angrily, "maybe Bob had a gun, maybe he didn't. But if he did, I wouldn't have had any way to get to it."

"I don't follow you."

"Bob didn't let anyone behind the bar. Ever," Grif explained. "His wife, Gloria and the bartender were the only people he let get within ten feet of the cash register, which happened to be behind the bar."

"Who tended bar back then?" J.D. asked.

Shrugging, Grif said, "Two or three different guys that I remember. Bartenders come and go. Just ask your mother."

"Anyone you remember that didn't go?"

Grif shook his head. "Just that jerk Cal."

"Cal have a last name?"

Grif walked over to the collection of photographs and tapped a weathered, slightly arthritic finger against one of the images. "That's him there. Cal Matthews. Owns his own place now. He's a real back-stabbing s.o.b."

"And he's the guy you were arguing with at our wedding."

"I couldn't believe he had the nerve to show up there," Grif said disgustedly. "Cal's the reason Tory's mother is like she is. He never missed an opportunity to taunt her about Bob's affair. After Bob disappeared, he was the first one to suggest that he'd run off with Gloria."

"Did you buy that?" J.D. asked.

"Naw," Grif scoffed. "Bob was just having one of those midlife crisis things. He adored Tory. If he was going to run off with a waitress, he would have taken his daughter with him."

"Sorry," Tory said as she came into the room. "I had a hard time finding it." She handed the neatly rolled poster to Grif, then turned to J.D. and asked, "What are all those blueprints doing in your trunk?"

"I think I mentioned I had other clients."

Placing the barely touched bottle of beer on a cluttered end table, J.D. waited for Grif to thank Tory for the gift before he announced they were leaving.

"So," she said, clearly annoyed as she brusquely snapped the seat belt into the latch. "Did I give you enough time for your interrogation?"

"Yep."

"And after talking to Grif, can we mark him off the list of suspects?"

"I think so."

"What's that supposed to mean?"

"It means I don't think he killed your father. But," J.D. continued, "I also think he has some suspicions of his own."

"He liked my dad," Tory informed him. "I don't recall a cross word between them."

"But you were only a kid."

"Yes, I was a child," Tory retorted. "But I wasn't Helen Keller."

"Good," he said as he headed for the condo. "Then I take it that means you can follow a recipe."

"A recipe for what?"

"Food."

"What kind of food?"

"I haven't decided yet."

She continued to pester him all the way home, but J.D. wasn't about to satisfy her curiosity—at least not until they were standing face-to-face. For some reason, he wanted to see her reaction.

"If you won't tell me what I have to cook, will you at least tell me why?"

Tossing his keys on the table near the door, J.D. ignored the blinking red light on the answering machine and wrapped his arms around her, pulling her close as he leaned on the edge of the table.

He was instantly trapped in the seductiveness of her deep blue eyes. Lacing his fingers behind her back, J.D. took a few seconds just to enjoy the soft feel of her body against his. He also enjoyed the fact that she hadn't tensed, hadn't resisted this unplanned move in the least.

"You're cooking dinner tomorrow night," he told her.

"And you don't trust me enough to put together a meal from the food pyramid?"

He recognized the use of humor as her way of hiding nervousness. Swallowing a curse, J.D. pulled her even closer. Bending his head, he pressed his lips to hers, mentally reminding himself to go slow and easy. A task not easily accomplished since his desire for this woman was nearing an intolerable level.

His tongue teased the seam of her mouth until her lips parted, allowing him to explore the warm recesses of her mouth. He deepened the kiss, no longer hearing the mantra of slow-and-easy in his mind.

His body's response to the sweet, minty taste of her was immediate and enough to do the one thing he had been trying to avoid. He felt her hands begin to push against his chest.

"I'm not going to do anything but kiss you," he managed to say in a hoarse whisper.

"But we shouldn't—"

"I know we shouldn't," he interrupted. "But I can't seem to help myself, Tory."

He showered her face with innocent kisses, nibbled her earlobe and ran his lips along the side of her throat until he heard her soft moan. He could feel her taut nipples pressing against his chest as she slid her arms around to knead the muscles in his back. It was more than enough encouragement for J.D.

He found her slightly parted lips and nearly drowned in the heady sensations caused by the openness of her response. Her fingers began to massage his shoulders and he felt her move closer, until his aroused body pressed deeply against her stomach. This time, he was the one who let out a moan.

Of course the telephone rang. J.D. lifted his mouth away from hers only long enough to say, "Let the machine get it."

She nodded, looking up at him through half-closed eyes. J.D.'s hand had just begun to explore the outline of her rib cage beneath one full breast when the machine began taping the message. The unmistakable voice drew them apart almost instantly.

"Did you like the present I sent you, Tory?" came the cruel, mocking voice. "Did you know it was buried at the Rusty Nail all this time. I dug it up before they started working on the dependency. Be a good girl, Tory. That isn't the only gun in the world."

Chapter Fifteen

"Damn," J.D. bellowed. He grabbed the phone but it was too late. The caller had apparently already hung up.

She stood very still as J.D. worked the machine to replay the stored messages. The first three were hang-ups. The fourth was from a Mrs. Bradford Willingham of the Charleston Ladies Trust Foundation.

"Why don't you take a long soak in the tub. Then you can call Mrs. Blue-blood when you're more relaxed," J.D. suggested.

"Do you think the hang-ups were the creepy caller?"

He shrugged and she could tell he was trying his best to be nonchalant about the whole matter. "Go soak," he repeated. "I'll bring you a glass of wine."

"In the tub?"

The grin he offered could be described as nothing short of wolfish. "I promised that minister I'd take care of you."

"I don't think invading my bath was what he had in mind when he asked that of you."

"There's a jar of some bubble-making stuff next to the faucet. You can cover yourself with bubbles and I promise I won't peek."

Said the spider to the fly.

Tory poured so much of the lilac-scented liquid into the tub that she actually had to let some of the water out. Still, she knew J.D. would have to have X-ray vision to see her through the blanket of bubbles. That should have made her happy. But it didn't. The menacing voice on the answering machine had scared her. But for some reason, her attraction to J.D. was even more frightening, though on a completely different level. As had happened at the wedding, all her principles and her sense of reason flew right out the window whenever he kissed her.

Touching her lips, Tory closed her eyes, allowing her mind to linger on the vivid memory of his kiss. No, she thought, *kiss* wasn't the right word to describe what J.D. did to her. It was like magic, defying any mundane description. All she knew was that what she felt for J.D. was far more complicated than simple lust. She'd lusted before. Lust she understood. But *this,* this was more intense, more vehement. No matter what the circumstances, her awareness of him never seemed to dip much lower than surface level. Sinking lower into the fragrant water, Tory tried to find an appropriate name for what she felt. The man annoyed her with his arrogance, yet had made certain her ailing mother was at the wedding. He understandably wasn't thrilled with their sleeping arrangements, yet there were no recriminations. He could be as charming as ever, and Lord knew he was a man of great passions. Especially the passion he seemed to be able to ignite in her at the drop of a hat.

Her eyes flew open when a single word scrolled through her mind—*love.* "Impossible." She spoke the thought aloud. "Absolutely ridiculous. I'm certainly not dumb enough to fall for him."

"You fell?" his voice called from the bedroom.

"No," she called back, praying that was all he had heard of her thoughts.

Tory felt her cheeks grow hot and knew it had nothing to do with the temperature of the water. It was the result of seeing J.D. saunter into the massive room, balancing a tray in his left hand.

"Isn't champagne overdoing it a little?"

He pretended to be quite wounded by her comment. He even became theatrical and held his hand over his heart. "I can't recall ever having a woman complain when I brought her champagne—complete with strawberries."

Mindless of the warm water, Tory felt a sudden chill. "So this is some sort of ritual for you?"

Placing the tray on one of the steps leading to the tub, J.D. appeared to be unfazed by her remark. Like an expert wine steward, he popped the top from the bottle, plunked a ripe berry into each of the glasses and poured.

Her only indication that he wasn't quite as cool as his expression would have her believe was the slight tremor in his hand.

His eyes met and held hers for what felt like a century before he finally spoke. "Are you asking me about my past relationships?"

Yes . . . no . . . yes, her brain cried in utter confusion. "None of my business," she said as she sipped her drink.

"After that little bombshell you dropped on me yesterday, don't you think it's a little late for us to adopt a don't-ask don't-tell policy?"

Tory gulped the champagne. *I'm completely naked and having a conversation with a man about sex, while he's fully clothed and obviously much more comfortable with the subject.*

"I only told you about me because I thought you had figured it out on your own."

"I probably should have," he said with a lopsided grin. "And I'm sorry if I said or did anything in the Bahamas that made you feel pressured or uncomfortable."

"Having a conversation with you while I'm in the bathtub is making me very uncomfortable," she blurted out.

His eyes never left her face, but the sound of his deep, throaty chuckle echoed in the room. "One of the things I admire about you is your honesty, doll."

"Thanks," she managed to say. One of the things? she added mentally.

"I've had two fairly serious relationships in my life," he told her. "And I have never had unprotected sex, so you can scratch that concern off your list."

Tory considered drowning herself right then and there. "You're talking as if you think we're going to...going to..."

He shook his head and said, "I'm simply telling you this because I recognize the chemistry between us."

"Arguing over everything is chemistry?"

"We have a lot in common. First and foremost seems to be desire."

"Aren't you jumping to conclusions here?"

One dark eyebrow arched high on his forehead. "I would be happy to illustrate my point." He stood slowly, placing his glass on the tiles as his fingers went to his belt buckle.

"Wait!" she said, nearly coming out of the water.

J.D. resumed his position at the edge of the tub. "When I kiss you, I go out of my mind."

Was this J.D. Porter talking? she thought, blinking at the image of his handsome face.

"Why are you telling me this?"

His soft laughter held a certain amount of sadness. "Chalk it up to an attack of conscience."

"But you haven't done anything to feel guilty about," she assured him. "I'm the one who should be thanking you for marrying me. Now I can finish my Ph.D. You've been incredibly generous where my mother is concerned, and—"

"I didn't bring this subject up because I was interested in your gratitude," he interrupted.

She noted the tension in the set of his jaw and the slight pulsation of the veins at his temple.

"Then why?"

"I'm trying to tell you that I'll sleep on the couch for the duration."

"Thank you."

He was quiet long enough to drain his glass and refill it. "I want you to know, though..." His voice dropped an octave. "If you should change your mind, I'm very interested and more than willing to fulfill my husbandly duties."

He left the room. And left her wondering why the last portion of his statement had echoed the sadness that she had detected earlier. He was acting as if he was the villain, not her. She was the one reaping all the benefits from this marriage. Aside from making her eligible for the grant, J.D. had transformed her life into a fairy-tale existence. She was literally living in the lap of luxury.

"I'm drinking champagne in a damn tub big enough for a party," she grumbled. So why the hang-dog expression? she wondered. She couldn't believe it was because they hadn't consummated their arrangement. With his looks and charm, J.D. could easily find release in any one of a dozen clubs in the city.

"But he won't because he's married to you," she told her reflection as she stood drying herself with a large towel. Strange that it had taken her this long to realize that she'd married a very principled man. Even stranger was the fact that by the time she slipped on her robe, she was ready to admit to herself that she was falling in love with him.

She found him at the dining room table, the portable phone glued to his ear. She rinsed out the glasses and left them in the sink while he finished his call.

"I'll fly down some time next week and we can go over the plans then," he said before hanging up. He was in the act of lowering the antenna when she came and stood in front of him. The scent of lilac clung to her, filling the small space between them.

"I guess you should call that woman back about your grant."

"I will," she told him. "But first I..." she faltered. "I... what I'm trying to say is..."

"What do you want?" he asked, fighting to keep his hopes in check. Not to mention his body's immediate reaction as his eyes dropped and he realized she was naked beneath the short silk robe. "What do you want?" he repeated with more force. He silently swore he'd throw himself off the balcony if she didn't give the right answer—the only answer as far as he was concerned.

"You," she whispered, color faintly staining her cheeks.

J.D. was momentarily paralyzed—except for the part of him that was reacting solely to the implications of her suggestion. "I told you I didn't want your gratitude."

"This has nothing to do with gratitude," she said as she extended both delicate hands and placed them on his shoulders.

In the process, she moved so that her supple body moved in between his parted thighs. He heard the small gasp when she was pressed fully against him. If she thought that was hard, he'd gladly trade places with her. He ached like a teenager but was man enough to know he would have to exercise infinite patience and tenderness with her. He also knew she might call it quits at any time.

His fingers circled her waist, pulling her firmly against his rigid shaft. He met her wide blue eyes with his own. "If you're not sure, please tell me now," he said—rather pleaded, that was a better description for the way the words were wrenched from his intensely excited body.

With him seated, they were eye level. He saw the full range of emotions in her expression—curiosity, uncertainty—but uppermost, he saw desire in those thickly lashed eyes.

Please, he prayed silently.

As if answering his unspoken plea, Tory brushed her lips against his, tentatively at first. J.D. reined in the fierce desire surging through him and allowed her to set the pace. When she grew bolder, more assured, he allowed his hands to slowly move up her sides. He felt her shiver and heard her groan as her lips parted and they began that time-tested sparring of tongues that fanned the flames of his long-checked need.

The outline of each rib brought him closer and closer to his true goal. Tory ground her hips against his with the first brush of his thumb over her distended nipple. He moved confidently then, cupping the underside of her breast in one hand, grasping the back of her neck with the other. He longed to strip the silk away from her skin, yet he didn't dare do anything that might cause her to pull back. Even though it was killing him, he continued to exercise restraint.

As his palm applied pressure to her breast, she smiled. He could feel it. He could also feel her legs trembling against his. If it was going to happen, he thought as he lifted her into his arms, it was going to happen right.

Carrying her to the bedroom, J.D. gently placed Tory on the bed and fell into place beside her. "Are you sure?" he whispered huskily.

"Very," she answered without hesitation.

It took very little effort to untie the belt of her robe. Bracing himself on one elbow, J.D. simply stared down at her with a sense of awe and appreciation he had never felt for any other woman.

"You're beautiful."

She moaned at his compliment, a little catching of breath that caused her breasts to rise along with his blood pressure. Tory was all softness and curves. She was what a woman was supposed to be, he thought as he shrugged out of his shirt.

The golden and pink light of the sunset cast allur-
ing shadows across her inviting body. Tossing aside the
remainder of his clothing, J.D. became intent upon
using his fingertips to trace a sensual path from the
tight indentation of her navel to the deep valley between her breasts. He was aware of her passiveness,
but somehow he knew it wasn't disinterest.

"Touch me," he said, pressing his open mouth
against her warm forehead.

Her feather-light exploration was far more erotic
than anything he had ever imagined. Her nails wove
through the mat of hair on his chest and toyed with his
pebble-hard nipple. Watching her fingertips move over
his body caused a deep, heartfelt groan of pure pleasure to rumble from his throat.

"Let me take this off," he said, lifting her slightly
to free her arms from the robe. He also used the opportunity to partially cover her body with his, feeling
her sink into the soft mattress. Tory's legs were
smooth and sent electric tingles shooting through his
system when she rubbed her bare thigh the full length
of his.

He kissed her for a long time, mostly to keep from
exploding right then and there. She tasted so sweet,
smelled so feminine, he was really struggling to maintain control.

Easing his lips away from hers, J.D. pressed his
mouth against her nipple, experiencing her skin. And
it was an experience—one that very nearly had him
going out of his mind. When he began to pull away, he
felt her hands at the back of his head.

"That feels good," she purred. "So good."

The trancelike effect in her tone worked like a nar-
cotic, sending him even closer toward personal re-

lease. Somehow, J.D. managed to hold himself in check as he explored her writhing body. Slowly, carefully, he learned what she liked and what she didn't; what she was comfortable with, and what made her small frame tense. She seemed unable or, he hoped, incapable of hiding her reactions to the things she liked.

For reasons he didn't bother to analyze, he wanted this experience to be fabulous for her. To be magic.

Tory apparently had some ideas of her own on the subject. Her fingers sought and found the sensitive skin at his inner thigh. She never actually touched him, but she didn't have to. It was pure pleasure just to be taunted with the knowledge that her fingers were a mere fraction of an inch from his hardness. She varied the pressure, occasionally digging her nails into his skin, especially when he took her nipple into his mouth.

He wanted this to go on forever, but he knew it was impossible. He lay back on the bed, rolling her with him in the process. Easing his hand between their perspiration-drenched bodies, J.D. gently massaged her as she straddled his body.

''Please,'' she said against his mouth, moving her hips in a downward motion.

He bent his head and touched the very tip of one breast. Summoning the reserves of his control, J.D. gently slid inside her, then went very still.

Meeting her eyes, he felt instantly relieved when he saw nothing but raw passion and expectation. They moved together, slowly at first, then more urgently. J.D. touched her intimately while his other hand gripped the side of her hip. He liked her being on top, it made it possible for him to ensure that her fulfillment happened.

Though it nearly killed him, he waited until he felt the gentle contractions seize her before he allowed his own release.

Moments later, Tory lay with her head against his chest, her eyes half-closed, her body still linked with his in the most primitive of ways. Wrapped in his arms and a contentment she had never before experienced, she listened as his heartbeat slowed and returned to a normal rhythm. His deep, even breaths washed over her still-damp skin, though she wasn't cold. She was too filled with a sense of awe to be cold.

"It wasn't supposed to be like that," she said.

"You're an expert?" he teased, rubbing his callused hand across her bottom.

Giving several of the hairs on his chest a sharp tug, Tory said, "I mean for me. It wasn't supposed to be like that for *me.*"

"And where did you pick up this bit of information?"

"Girl talk."

"And how old were these girls when they told you having sex was going to be bad for you?"

Tory lifted her head and met his amused gray gaze. "Haven't you ever heard the expression, 'Just close your eyes and think of England'?"

"You weren't thinking of England."

"You got that right," she agreed, moving and snuggling into the crook of his arm. "I'm not sure how we got on the subject of England, but I was trying to tell you that—"

"It was good for you?" he finished.

"Yeah."

"I'm glad," he said as he moved to lace his fingers so that she was locked in his embrace. "I was terrified."

"Of what?"

"I've never done this before."

Playfully, she slapped the corded muscles of his stomach. "Right."

"I mean I've done *that*. I've just never done it... I've never been anyone's first time, is what I meant."

His apparent nervousness made her smile. "Can't bring yourself to say the 'V' word, eh, J.D.?"

"You're making this very hard, Victoria."

"I was simply offering a compliment, Joseph," she said, matching his tone.

"Well," he stammered. "Thanks."

Tory began to laugh when she looked up to see the bright red stains on his cheeks. "Why are you embarrassed?"

"Why don't you go call Mrs. Blue-blood before it gets too late," he answered, a sudden hardness in his tone.

She sensed that the sudden change had nothing to do with her laughing. But seeing the complexity of conflicting emotions turning his eyes that glistening silver was definitely not a good sign. "What's wrong?"

"Nothing."

"I'm sorry I laughed."

"Nothing's wrong," he nearly yelled.

Perplexed, Tory tried to decipher the sudden change in him. "Something *is* wrong."

"Leave it alone, Tory. I said nothing was wrong."

On that less than pleasant note, J.D. bounded from the bed and moved toward the bathroom. Pausing at the doorway, he spoke with his back to her. "Don't commit yourself to anything for tomorrow night. You're cooking, remember?"

Almost desperate to draw him back into amiable conversation, she asked, "Are you going to tell me what I'm cooking? Or for whom?"

"I invited my mother to dinner."

Chapter Sixteen

"He actually called me his mother?" Rose gushed, her eyes glistening with tears.

"Those were his exact words," Tory promised. *And the last ones he said to me all flaming evening,* she added mentally.

"You swear you didn't talk him into this?" Rose persisted.

"Come on. You know J.D. I couldn't talk him into dousing himself with water if he was standing in front of me in flames."

Rose eyed her closely. "Is that what the two of you are fighting about?"

"Who says we're fighting?" Tory hedged.

"You bolted in here like the devil was chasing you the minute J.D. parked the car."

"The devil wasn't chasing me," Tory corrected with a sad smile. "He married me."

Rose looked positively crestfallen. "Is it really that bad between the two of you?"

Taking her lower lip between her teeth, Tory mentally replayed her relationship with her husband. "It's either incredibly wonderful or pure hell. The man obviously doesn't believe in middle ground."

"Just discovering that, are you?" Wes asked as he joined them in the office above the restaurant.

Why couldn't J.D. be more like his brother? Tory wondered. Wes was always so relaxed, always on an even keel. She bet he never gave in to his anger—or his passion.

Tory swallowed as the memory came rushing to her consciousness with enough vividness to cause a stirring in the pit of her stomach. No, she couldn't imagine feeling the way she felt with any man but J.D. Worse yet, she didn't want to. She'd accepted that fact before she'd taken the initiative the night before. Temper and all, she loved J.D.

"If it's any consolation," Wes began, "he doesn't seem any happier than you are."

"Good," Tory responded. "Because he's the one with the problem, not me."

"Want to tell me about it?"

Tory gave Wes a sidelong glance. "No."

Wes grinned. "Neither did J.D. Which tells me a lot."

"I don't think you're helping, Wesley," Rose interjected. "Whatever the trouble is between the two of them is their business. Not ours."

Tory watched as Wes and Rose exchanged a look. Well, she amended, maybe it wasn't so much a look as some sort of silent communication she wasn't meant to understand.

"Tell me about Gloria, the waitress," Tory said.

"Not much to tell," Rose said with a shrug. "Just before your dad...disappeared, Gloria took off for someplace out West. Vegas or Reno, I think."

"She left before my father was killed?" Tory asked.

"By a day or so. I remember because she didn't hang around for payday." Rose's eyebrows came together as she appeared to be searching her memory. "But we didn't have a payday. Your dad disappeared and so did all the cash."

"I know my father..." Tory halted in midsentence, suddenly putting bits and pieces together. "When my father left, my mother and I had to go and live with my grandmother because he had cleaned out the bank accounts. But if he didn't leave..."

"What happened to the money?" Rose finished for her. "It wasn't here at the bar, I can promise you that. What little bit was in the cash register, Cal kept for himself."

"Did the money disappear before or after Gloria left town?" Tory asked.

"That I don't know," Rose answered. "And Brewster didn't keep many of the old bookkeeping records when he took the place over from Cal."

"What's Gloria's last name?"

"I'll have to think about that," Rose said with a sigh. "It wasn't like she and I were the best of friends, if you get my drift."

"Maybe Cal knows," Wes suggested. "Can you get in touch with him?"

"You could almost walk to his restaurant from here," Tory explained.

"Is it a nice place?"

"Very," Tory stated emphatically. "Prime real estate in the center of the historic district. I've seen block-long lines on Friday and Saturday nights."

"Well," Wes said as he fiddled with a ring of plastic keys that Chad had probably left behind, "I suggest you invite your husband out to lunch."

"What do I need him for?" Tory responded, fairly certain J.D. would starve before he'd accept an invitation from her.

Wesley was quiet for a minute, then as diplomatically as possible, he said, "Even in a city as quaint as Charleston, there is the occasional threatening person. Generally speaking, I think it's always better for women to go out in groups these days."

"You and I could be a group," she told her brother-in-law.

Wes shook his head violently. "The last time I took something of my brother's without asking permission, I ended up having my two front teeth capped."

"And they aren't permanent caps," J.D. said as his large form filled the doorway.

J.D.'s jeans and shirt held the telltale signs of hands-on work on the dependency. Tory could easily make out the imprint of where he had wiped his hands on the front of his jeans. Some of his ebony hair had fallen forward and she longed to go to him and tenderly put it right. She would also rather remove her own spleen with an oyster fork before she'd make the first overture.

"What idiotic thing does she want to do?" he asked Wes.

"J.D. Porter!" Rose shouted. "Don't speak about your wife as if she wasn't standing three feet from you."

Rose's reprimand worked because J.D. looked at her for the first time. It did not, however, remove the distant look in his hooded gray eyes. "So tell me."

"I want to go see Cal Matthews," she explained. After filling him in on their discussion about the money and the odd sequence of events at the time of her father's murder, J.D. became the concerned, attentive husband again.

"I'll go home and catch a quick shower," he told her. "Please go down and explain how to use the heat gun to the subcontractor so the workers don't burn down the building while we're having lunch."

"Why me?" she asked.

"You're supposed to be the preservationist around here. So unless you want that seventeen-year-old apprentice singeing the cypress moldings, I suggest you go and demonstrate the proper way to remove the paint and plaster."

"Fine," she said, staring him directly in the eye, refusing to be humbled.

"You," she heard him say to his brother, "are not invited to join us."

"Jealousy is a very unhealthy offshoot of a very healthy emotion called—"

"Remember your caps, little brother."

"Right," Wes answered and she could hear the amusement in his response.

J.D. WAS BACK, smelling wonderfully fresh and looking sexier than ever in a pale green shirt and chinos. Tory was still working with the young man as she watched his approach. Swagger, she thought. The man swaggered.

"And don't forget to wear the mask," she reminded the boy for the third time.

"Sure thing, Tory," he responded in a slow, uneducated accent.

"Mrs. Porter," J.D. thundered at the lanky kid. Then, turning to her, he asked, "Ready?"

"Yes."

"Don't screw that up," he told the boy as he led her out of the building and across the pathway of sand-encrusted plywood.

"Are you always so impolite to your employees?" she asked as soon as they were inside the car.

"Only when I catch them leering at my wife."

"Leering?"

"That kid was staring at you like you were the first woman he'd ever seen."

Tory slumped against the seat and directed a disgusted breath in the direction of her bangs. "Correct me if I'm wrong," she began in a tentative voice, "but I thought having sex would be a bonus for you."

"It complicates things," he said.

What was I expecting? she asked herself angrily. "Only for me," she retorted. "You've been an absolute ogre ever since."

"We shouldn't have done it."

Tory wasn't sure what hurt more, the fact that he had regrets, or the determination with which he'd voiced his lamentations.

Her defense mechanisms kicked in. "I thought it was supposed to be the woman who regretted it in the morning."

J.D. didn't look at her, even though he could have. They were stuck in a long line of unmoving traffic.

"It still shouldn't have happened. At least not yet."

"Right," Tory retorted smartly. "We definitely should have waited until we were married." In a display of purely childish anger, she wriggled her hand in front of his face, all but jabbing him in the eye with her wedding band.

"I meant, we shouldn't have acted on our feelings until everything is resolved," J.D. told her through gritted teeth.

"Greer will eventually solve my father's murder, if possible. And maybe Cal Matthews can tell me enough about this Gloria person so that I can find out why she took all my family's money."

"Why are you so sure Gloria took the money?"

"She's the only one that left town," Tory reasoned. "I believe there's a saying about 'take the money and run.'"

"Are you some sort of dictionary of quaint sayings?"

"I'm only trying to tell you that if your regrets are because my father's murder is unsolved, it will pass. So there's no reason for you to continue to treat me like I'm a thorn in your side."

"What about the calls? What about the kook who's been threatening you?"

Tory shivered at the mere thought. "Once the murder is solved, I'm sure the calls will stop. So what other issues do you think need resolving between us?"

It was like watching the gates close against a flood. J.D.'s face became a blank palette from which she could pull no color.

Tory sighed again. "I talked to Mrs. Willingham last night and she seemed to think I was a shoo-in for the grant. I'll get my degree." *And I'll lose you.*

"That should make you happy," he said, obviously trying to keep his voice even and emotionless.

"It will," she assured him.

J.D. parked next to a fancy Jaguar in the half-full lot across from the restaurant uncreatively named Cal's Place. He walked at her side but was very careful not to touch her. Disheartening didn't even begin to describe the way she was feeling when they stepped inside the art-deco interior of the restaurant.

"Nice place," he commented. "Very deceptive from the outside. Great use of interior space."

"Maybe they'll let you skim the blueprints instead of a menu," Tory suggested with a snide smile as they waited at the hostess stand.

"I was just mentioning it because the place obviously had to be gutted. It's expensive to gut a building and maintain the outside facade."

"I know. I saw what you're charging Rose and Shelby, remember?"

"Two?" a blonde in a low-cut white dress asked.

"Please."

J.D. and Tory were seated beneath a neon objet d'art that amounted to a bright splash of pink and green that seemed to have absolutely no meaning.

The hostess handed them their menus and said, "Your server will be right with you."

"We'd like to see the manager," Tory announced.

The woman's expression grew perplexed. "If there's a problem, I can—"

"I know Cal," Tory cut in. "Just tell him Victoria Conway is here. I'd just like to say a quick hello."

The woman visibly relaxed and disappeared down a corridor with a large Exit sign dangling from the high ceiling above.

She reappeared after a short time and scurried over as quickly as her Lycra dress would allow. "Cal's not in right now, but I'll be sure and let him know you stopped by."

"I'll leave my home numb—"

"That's fine," J.D. interrupted, placing his hand over hers where she had begun to write on the cocktail napkin. "We'll stop in again. Maybe we can catch him then."

When the hostess walked away from the table, Tory turned to look at her husband, hostility radiating from every cell in her body. "How am I supposed to find Gloria if I don't talk to Cal?"

"Cal won't return your call," he said with complete confidence.

"And how do you know that?"

"Remember the Jag we parked next to?"

Tory nodded.

"The car belongs to Cal. I saw him get into it after his chat with Grif at our wedding."

"So you think he's really here and just avoiding me?"

J.D. shook his head. "My guess is he's bolted out the back way, just in case you became insistent."

It appeared that J.D. had been right. After a very fast meal, they returned to find the spot next to the Mercedes unoccupied.

As if sensing her disappointment, J.D. draped his arm over her shoulder and gave her a quick but much-needed hug. "I'll bet Sweaty Evan knows her name."

Tory instantly perked up. "If he was keeping the books, he'd have to have written her paychecks."

"Let's give him a call," J.D. suggested.

As soon as they were back at the condo, Tory did just that. They'd made a stop at the market to get what she needed to fix dinner.

She slammed the phone down for the third time. "According to Margaret, he's still *unavailable*."

"Seems to me like you're being sandbagged, doll."

"Sandblasted is more like it," she grumbled in frustration. "And I'd love to call Greer, but I'm afraid the creepy caller will get wind of it and I couldn't stand another one of his threatening calls."

"Grif?" J.D. suggested.

"He has more Dewars in his veins than blood," she told him. "If your mother can't remember Gloria's last name, I doubt Grif will be much help."

"You won't know until you try."

Tory nodded and dialed the number. "Hi," she said as soon as he answered. "I need to know Gloria's last name," she said without preamble.

"What are you up to?"

"I'm not up to anything," Tory explained, wondering if Grif's voice really did have a hesitancy to it or if she was just paranoid from an entire day of being put off.

"Let the cops do their thing, Tory."

J.D. must have seen the surprise in her expression as she gaped at the receiver. "Grif, why are you doing this tap dance?" She could see J.D. close his eyes and shake his head sadly, but right then she was more interested in why her longtime friend was suddenly skirting a direct question.

"I think you need to let the police do their job and stay out of it."

"Come clean," she said sternly. "What do you know?" Her question was answered with dead silence. "I swear, Grif, if you don't tell me why you've suddenly changed sides, I'll be on your doorstep in less than fifteen minutes. And I'll bring J.D. with me."

"I don't think you understand," Grif said.

"No," she agreed. "I don't understand why you're acting this way. I'm not asking you for the location of your secret fishing spot. All I want is one flaming last name.''

''Burrows.''

''Thank you,'' she said.

''Take my advice, Tory. Let this alone.''

''Why?''

''Because I have a bad feeling about this. Too many people are running around with their dander up. Evan told me about your visit, and apparently the cops are leaning on him pretty good.''

''I hope they are,'' Tory told him. ''If he's the one that killed my father.''

''It wasn't Evan.''

''How do you know that?''

''You forget,'' he said in a grim, almost sorrowful voice. ''I know all the players here. Evan isn't a killer.''

''Then you apparently have never been to his office.''

Tory was saddened at the uncomfortable end to her conversation with Grif. She valued his friendship but resented his vehement opposition to her need to find Gloria.

J.D. had already begun to prepare the skewers of chicken and vegetables when she joined him in the kitchen. After recounting her conversation with Grif, she asked, ''Why were you shaking your head before?''

''Because I thought your friend Grif was on the level.''

''He did give me Gloria's last name. I'll call Greer and see if he can track her down for me.''

J.D.'s mirthless laughter didn't exactly improve her mood.

"What?"

"Even when Greer gets around to finding Gloria—
which he probably will—it won't be for the purpose of
providing *you* with that information."

Tory's spine stiffened as she stood wielding the half-
full skewer like a sword. "Then I'll go to the library
and hunt through every phone book until I find her."

"If you want to waste your time," he said with a
shrug.

"Forgive me, sire. As usual, you must have a better suggestion?"

A smile tugged at the corners of his mouth as he
turned to face her. "As a matter of fact, I do. Dylan
Tanner."

Taken aback for a moment, Tory had to admit his
plan made a hell of a lot more sense. "I apologize for
being a snot," she said, getting up on tiptoe to place a
kiss against his cheek. "I'll just run back to the phone
and do some of my best groveling to Dylan."

DINNER WITH ROSE could only be described as
strained, in Tory's opinion. Funny, she thought as she
cleared the dishes from the table, Rose was really
working hard at winning J.D. over. At the moment,
J.D.'s mother was drawing him into conversation
about the work on the dependency when the phone
rang.

"I'll get it," Tory called, racing into the bedroom
for two reasons. First, she wanted desperately to keep
anything from interrupting the reunion of mother and
son. Second, she hoped it might be Dylan with news
about Gloria.

"You don't listen well, Tory."

The blood seemed to stop pumping from her heart at the now-familiar, hoarse voice on the other end.

"I don't know what you're talking about."

"I told you to stay out of it. You've left me no other choice. I'm going to have to kill you."

Chapter Seventeen

Shaking, Tory was racing back down the hallway when the first snippets of J.D.'s deep voice broke through the barrier of fear.

"...have her mother declared legally incompetent. I've already contacted an attorney and she's drawing up the papers."

"And that will give you and Tory clear title to the Rose Tattoo?"

"As husband and wife, it shouldn't be a problem. Everything is going according to your plan."

"My mother still owns the Rose Tattoo?" Tory gasped, glaring at J.D. "You manipulative son of a bitch." She then looked at her boss with equal contempt. "You planned this all out? I can't believe you'd do something like this to me."

J.D. jumped to his feet and took a step in her direction. Tory held up her hand as she groped behind her for her purse and keys. "I hope you and your mother enjoy dessert. The only difference between the two of you," she said as tears began to flow freely down her cheeks, "is that J.D. kissed me first."

"OF COURSE I've looked everywhere!" J.D. shouted at Wes. "I should have told her the truth from the start. It's what I wanted to do."

"I'm sorry I talked you out of it," Rose said, her shoulders slumped forward. "*I* was the manipulator, not you."

"But you didn't sleep with her," Wes commented.

J.D. stopped pacing and stared at his younger brother.

"And something tells me it wasn't your run-of-the-mill experience, either." Wes came over and placed a hand on his shoulder. "J.D., you've been wearing your guilt like an open wound ever since you said I do. But this morning, it was very obvious from the vibes between the two of you that you weren't playing in name only anymore."

Raking his fingers through his hair, J.D. cursed. "I've checked everyplace I can think of."

"Ashley Villas?"

"That was the first place I called. She isn't with her mother."

"My money says she is," Wes countered.

J.D. gave him a questioning look.

"People are generally predictable. Tory's normal pattern is to go and sit with her mother, where she feels safe."

"But I called," J.D. insisted.

"And if she was as upset as you two said, they probably lied to you in an effort to protect her. You're the one that told me the doctors and nurses are very close to her."

J.D. nodded and reached into the front pocket of his jeans.

"I think I should be the one to go," Wes said, taking a half step toward the door.

J.D. snorted. "She's my wife."

"Who probably hates you right now," Wes explained. "And you, too," he added to the solemn figure seated in the chair. "Let me take a shot at it. It's the least I can do for her."

J.D. thanked Wes by giving him a brotherly hug. "Just convince her to hear me out."

"I'll try. But I think this is something the two of you need to work out alone."

J.D. agreed. Facing his mother, he said, "I'll let you know what happens."

"But it was all my doing," Rose protested. "I should be the one to—"

"I think it's about time we heeded Wes's advice. We've screwed this up pretty badly."

"But there's more—"

"Mother," J.D. cut her off. "Go home. Wes, give her a call if you have any luck with Tory."

Rose looked as if she might protest, but J.D. gave her one final warning look that could have silenced a politician running for reelection and behind in the polls.

"IT'S YOU!" Tory yelped, clutching a small butter knife in her hand.

Wesley offered her an apologetic smile. "You seem to have a thing for greeting me with some sort of weapon in your hand."

Tory glanced down through a steady stream of tears at the object she clutched so tightly. "Sorry," she said. "I took the knife off one of the meal trays, just in case."

"I'm glad I came instead of J.D. I'd hate to think you're distraught enough to do him in." Wes stepped into the dimly lit room and sat in the chair on the opposite side of the room.

The figure in the bed gave no sign of awareness, but Tory was aware. "Brewster was obviously more than just a friend of Gramma's. He didn't really buy the Rusty Nail from you, did he, Mama? I've put the pieces together, and I take it that since my mother's been this way since my father died, the Rose Tattoo actually belongs to me. Or it will if I have my mother declared legally incompetent to manage her affairs."

Wes shook his head. "I'm not here to make J.D.'s excuses for him, Tory. That's between the two of you."

"There's nothing between the two of us," she told him in a small voice.

"I beg to differ. I know my brother. I've also just spent the last five hours watching him lose his mind wondering where you were."

Tory hung her head and closed her eyes, silently praying for some control over her emotions. It was slow in coming, but Wes was apparently a very patient man.

"The ironic part of all this," she began as she lifted her head, "is that I've been feeling guilty over J.D.'s being forced to marry me. And all this time, he and Rose were scheming and plotting."

"My mother plotted," Wes countered.

"I can understand that," Tory exclaimed. "I know how much the Tattoo means to her. I'm not thrilled that she used me instead of coming to me with the truth."

"The only time my mother has ever confronted anything directly was when she and my father were fighting for custody. She lost big time on that one."

"Okay. So she didn't think she could deal with me directly. Shelby could have."

"Shelby only owns half the bar."

"And when J.D. divorces me, he gets half of what I have."

"I think that was the original plan. But like I said, you and J.D. have to work this out."

"I don't see what there is to work out."

"Look me in the eye and tell me you aren't in love with him."

Tory managed to hold his gaze for a fraction of a second before her eyes dropped to the small, reflective blade of the knife she held.

"I thought so."

"Then you must realize that only makes matters worse."

"You'll never know until you try."

"It isn't that easy," she protested weakly, drained from the hours of emotional strain.

"You can deal with J.D. now," Wes suggested, "or you can spend the rest of your life wondering what might have been."

"I hate psychiatrists," Tory said.

"So does the rest of my family."

My family. She looked from Wes to the passive shell that was once her mother. It wasn't long before she was asking herself whether she wanted to spend her life alone, or try to work things out with J.D. The only other loving person in her life was Grif, but he wasn't exactly the demonstrative type.

She looked Wes directly in the eyes and asked, "Is J.D. in love with me?"

Wes's expression was benign. "If he is, he should be the one to tell you. Not me."

Tory was half out of the chair when she remembered the call. "I can't go back to the condo."

Wes regarded her for a long moment, then adjusted his glasses. "Why?" His head tilted toward the knife still in her hand.

"I got another call. He said he was going to kill me. If I'm with J.D., there's a chance that . . ."

"Good Lord!" Wes groaned. "You should have called the police and stayed in the apartment."

"Forgive me, but I didn't exactly feel very welcome when I learned my husband and my mother-in-law were screwing me."

"Point," Wes conceded. "Let me take you home in my car. We'll have security walk us out, and I'll arrange for J.D. to meet us at the elevator."

HE WASN'T at the elevator. J.D. was standing in the center of the parking lot as they pulled into a vacant spot.

"I've been half out of my mind," he said as soon as he opened the passenger door. Then, leaning into the car, he said to his brother, "I owe you."

Tory felt a surge of panic welling up inside and she looked at Wes, who simply shrugged.

"You're not coming up with us?"

"Not part of my duties as best man," he told her gently. "You're in control from here on out."

But she didn't feel in control. Especially not when she entered the condo with J.D. right on her heels. Dinner with Rose was a walk in the park compared to the tension that now filled every square inch of the apartment.

"I told them to tell you I wasn't there if you called." It was meant as neither an apology nor an explanation. It was just the only thing she could think of to break the unbearable silence.

"I don't know where to begin," J.D. said as he fell into a chair, cradling his head in his hands. "But I hope you know it was never my intention to hurt you in any way."

"Marrying me so that you'd be entitled to half my assets was accidental?"

"I didn't marry you because of the Rose Tattoo," he said, lifting his eyes to meet hers.

Tory nearly melted when she saw the dampness glistening on his inky lashes. "Then why?"

"I told myself I was doing it because I needed some way to show my mother I really had put the past behind us."

"You could have done that over dinner."

J.D. gave her a wry smile. "You aren't going to make this easy for me, are you?"

"Nope."

"I pretty much had myself convinced that I was going along with Rose's plan because *she* wanted me to."

"But?" Tory prodded, holding her breath as she anticipated his answer. It would either thrill her or destroy her on the spot. Realizing that only confirmed her earlier suspicions. In spite of everything, she loved him, unconditionally.

Tory never got an answer to her question because Dylan Tanner arrived unannounced. Dylan kept his visit brief and to the point. Gloria Burrows was in Las

Vegas, working as a cashier at some small casino off the main strip. After handing J.D. a slip of paper, which she assumed had all the information he'd related, Dylan left.

"I'd like to speak to Gloria Burrows, please," she heard J.D. say to the voice on the other end. "When will she be in?" There was a long pause before J.D. asked, "Do you know if I would be able to reach her at home? It's an urgent family matter."

A tingle of renewed wariness danced along her spine. J.D. was a fast and effective liar. Would she be able to trust him when and if he ever did get around to explaining his part in the deception? The question haunted her, along with the fear that surfaced each and every time her mind replayed the death threat from the creepy caller.

"My name is J. D. Porter, and she can reach me at this number." He rattled off the number with the area code. "Please make sure she gets the message."

J.D. glanced up from the phone and said, "I have a feeling she won't get the message."

"So now what?"

"Not to worry. Dylan provided her home number, as well."

"Let me call," Tory insisted. "You're a stranger. She'll probably blow you off. I'm a part of her past she'll have a harder time ignoring."

He vacillated for a moment, then dialed a number and handed her the phone.

On the third ring, a very groggy voice croaked, "Hello?"

"Is this Gloria Burrows?"

"Yes, and I was sleeping, if you don't mind!" the woman growled back. "How many times do I have to tell you stupid salespeople, I work nights and sleep during the day."

"This is Victoria Porter. But you'd remember me as Tory Conway."

The gasp on the other end was audible. Apparently, Gloria had a good memory.

Unfortunately, her demeanor didn't match her recall. "What the hell do you want?"

"I'm calling about my father's murder."

"It's a little late if you're expecting me to send flowers."

"I'm not interested in a bereavement gift, Ms. Burrows. I'm only concerned with what happened to the twenty-three thousand dollars that disappeared when you did."

The laugh at the other end of the phone evolved into a series of hacking, uncontrollable coughs that told her Gloria was probably a heavy smoker.

"I sure as hell didn't take it," Gloria said as soon as the coughing fit passed. "I left Charleston with nothing more than my clothes and my tips from my last night at work."

"Why the sudden departure?"

"Why do you care?" came the malicious retort.

"Because you were having an affair with my father and he's dead."

"I don't have to take this harassment," Gloria bellowed. "I'm sorry about your father—he was a decent little guy. But take my advice, honey. Leave the past where it is."

With that, Gloria slammed down the phone, leaving Tory to rub her injured ear and to deal with a very odd feeling gnawing at her.

"No luck, I take it," J.D. said.

"Either she's an accomplished liar, or something isn't right here."

"Meaning?"

It was hard to pinpoint her thoughts, especially when J.D. was standing close enough for her to feel the warmth emanating from his large body. *Was it really only last night that she'd lain snuggled in the comfort of his arms?*

"Gloria's reaction to hearing my father was dead. Either she already knew," Tory surmised, "or the torrid affair I've been hearing about wasn't all that torrid."

"My mother said it was pretty blatant, and she has no reason to lie to you."

Tory met his eyes, allowing her glowering expression to let him know what she thought of his remark.

"Not about the affair," he corrected as he shifted his weight from foot to foot.

"And if Gloria is working nights in a dive casino in Las Vegas, she obviously didn't go out West with a tidy nest egg."

"She could have blown the money her first day in town. That's pretty easy to do in a place like Vegas," J.D. said.

"So now what do we do?" she asked, allowing her arms to fall limply at her sides.

"You're the one always quoting from the book of inane sayings. How about the one where the mountain won't come to Mohammed?"

"You mean go to Nevada and see her?"

"At least we'll have a feel for what she's like. And maybe she can clarify the extent of her relationship with your father." J.D. placed his hands on either side of her head, effectively holding her between a rock and a hard place. Tory's only question was, which was which?

"If we go to Vegas, I'm pretty sure we'll get you away from the creepy caller. That's more important to me."

"Why?"

"Tory, I need for you to understand that I never meant to hurt you."

"Then you should never have lied to me."

Ducking under his arm, Tory went into the bedroom, locking the door behind her. She was exhausted. Too exhausted to deal with the very real possibility that J.D.'s motivation for marrying her probably had more to do with his inability to express his feelings to Rose than they did with her. Silent tears rolled onto the pillow until she finally drifted off into an empty sleep.

The next morning, J.D. was already in the process of making travel arrangements when she stumbled from the bedroom. She found some small satisfaction in the red puffiness around his eyes.

"Unless you want to fly all night, we've got to be at the airport in two hours."

"For what?"

"Las Vegas," he said as he placed a feather-light kiss on her opened mouth. "And hopefully a few answers."

THE MAN at the rental-car facility drew them detailed maps to Gloria's workplace as well as to her home. J.D. found the seedy casino with ease. Working their way through the maze of slot machines and computerized poker stations, they finally found the manager's office.

A man whose girth nearly matched his height glanced at them with general disinterest. "We're not hiring."

"We're not applying," J.D. told him. "We're looking for Gloria Burrows."

"Yeah?" he said. The unlit cigar plastered in one corner of his mouth bobbed as he spoke. "You and me both, pal. She didn't show for work this evening."

"Has someone been by her house to check on her?" Tory asked the repugnant little man.

"We don't check up on no-shows, honey. We fire 'em." He turned back to a stack of yellow invoices on his desk. "When you see Gloria, tell her not to bother coming in to pick up her check. I'll mail it."

"Interesting management style," J.D. commented as they left the casino.

"I don't know," Tory said with a smile. "He kind of reminded me of a short, fat version of you."

"Cute. Let's go see why Gloria just decided to commit professional suicide."

Her home was a dingy second-floor walk-up that made Tory's apartment look like a palace. "You wait here while I go see what's what."

"Why should I do that?" Tory argued.

"My instincts are telling me that something is very wrong here. I'd just feel better if you stayed in the car while I checked it out."

"Fine," she relented, knowing the sooner he got to Gloria, the sooner she could get out of this dry, oppressive heat.

His gut reaction that something was drastically wrong was confirmed the instant he saw the partially opened door to apartment 206. Careful not to disturb the knob, J.D. pushed the door open and found Gloria—lying in a pool of blood and moaning softly.

Chapter Eighteen

J.D. felt her pulse or, rather, the weak version thereof. Cursing softly, he grimaced at the gaping gash at the back of her skull. His first instinct was to grab the phone and dial 911, but then he didn't dare chance contaminating the crime scene.

"Tory!" he yelled down from over the warped wooden railing of the balcony.

"Can I come up now?"

"Go across the street to that package goods store and tell them to get the police and an ambulance over here now!"

After a rather lengthy interrogation by the state investigators, J.D. had about reached his boiling point. Tory was very quiet through it all. He assumed it was because of the huge bloodstain in the center of the matted beige carpet.

"I'm sure you have your own way of doing things," J.D. said to the officer in charge. "You've got to at least check out any possible connection between Ms. Burrows's injury and the murder in Charleston."

The plain-clothed investigator didn't appear to be too impressed by J.D.'s amateur speculations. "I hate to burst your bubble, Mr. Porter, but Ms. Burrows isn't a stranger to us. We haven't seen her in a couple of years, but she used to work the streets. It's probably nothing more than a trick gone bad.''

"There's a redial button," he heard Tory exclaim.

"What?"

"You said there was no sign of forced entry, right?" Tory asked the detective.

He nodded.

"If she called him and invited him to come here, then if you press the redial button on her phone, you'll know who she spoke to before..." Her voice trailed off and J.D. placed his arm around her waist.

"Has it been dusted?" the detective asked one of the other police officials.

The man nodded, then pressed redial. The long series of tones indicated a long-distance call.

"Hi. You've reached Cal's Place on Market Street. We're open Monday through—"

"Damn!" J.D. cursed as the recorded message continued. Catching Tory's chin between his thumb and forefinger, he lifted her face to his. "She must have called him after she talked to you yesterday." J.D. provided Greer's name and went into some additional details regarding the disappearance of Bob Conway. "I'm going to take my wife home on the first available flight," he added, almost daring the other man to tell him otherwise. "You can reach us at any of these numbers." He produced a business card and wrote additional numbers on the back. When he looked up, he found Tory had disappeared from the room. Alarmed, he called her name.

"In here."

Following the sound of her voice, J.D. joined her in what was obviously the bedroom. In her hand she held a framed picture and, judging by the hurt expression on her face, he immediately assumed it was a lurid picture of her father and Gloria. He was wrong.

Actually, he amended, as he stood behind his shaken wife, it was a lurid picture, but the man wasn't Bob Conway. It was Evan Richards.

"Judging by the clothes they're wearing, I'd guess this was taken around the time your father was murdered."

"Then why did she call Cal's restaurant?"

"I'll have them pass this on to Greer. Maybe the Charleston police can sort it all out by the time we fly home."

J.D. gave the photograph and an explanation to the investigator, reminding him to keep them informed.

"We've spoken to Greer, and Cal Matthews hasn't shown up yet. They're posting a patrol car at his restaurant to greet him." The investigator turned his back and barked a whole slew of instructions to the various people at the scene.

Tory was as nonconversational on the trip to the airport as she had been during the long flight to Nevada. J.D. felt himself grimace at the thought of another long period of silent confinement. What he and Tory needed was privacy. He had to find a way to make her understand his reasons for marrying her before her hatred sank so deep that the chance would be lost forever.

"I'm going to get a soda while you arrange for the tickets," she told him.

"No thanks, I'm not thirsty," he said under his breath as she took one of the escalators.

"Beverage service is complimentary on all our flights, sir," the ticket agent said, obviously oblivious to his predicament.

"Thanks," J.D. responded automatically.

THE FLIGHT was going to be pure unadulterated hell, she thought as she tore the paper wrapper from the straw and inserted it into the small opening of the plastic lid on the overpriced soft drink. Still, to quench her thirst, she would have whipped out her handy Gold Card.

"You really are stupid," the voice said from behind her.

Tory turned and discovered with shock that she was looking into a face from her past—the face of Calvin Matthews.

Acting on pure instinct, she tossed the contents of the soda at his face. Unfortunately, the lid failed to come off, so all that she managed to do was bounce a souvenir plastic cup off her tormentor.

Cal gripped her upper arm, his fingers biting into her flesh hard enough to make her wince. "I know your husband is up at the ticket counter. If you scream, or do anything to draw attention to us, I'll cut you and then go do the same to him."

Tory nodded, too paralyzed with fear for any vocal reply. Her brain was working a mile a minute as she allowed him to lead her through the crowded airport. Think! she repeated, until an idea finally bubbled to the surface.

Slowly and silently, she unsnapped her purse, all the while keeping her attention riveted to her captor. Operating by feel alone, Tory slid her school photo identification card out of its compartment and allowed it to slip from her fingers without Cal's noticing. Or, thankfully, any of the rushed tourists and conventioneers passing them along the way. If just one person commented on her tactic, she knew the sharp blade she could feel pressing against her skin would become more than just a threat.

One by one, Tory left a trail that included her library card, her driver's license, even her "Get Your Eleventh Pair of Panties Free" card from her favorite lingerie shop. She literally had one card left to play. She only hoped someone would follow her trail.

"In here," Cal growled against her ear.

Just before he shoved her into the room marked Utility Room—Do Not Enter, she flicked the last card onto the floor.

An eerie and intimidating quiet engulfed them. She could no longer hear the din of conversation or the ringing of the slot-machine bells. She was aware only of the sound of their footsteps against the metal catwalk that seemed to span the entire length of the airport. It also appeared to be completely deserted.

"Why are you doing this?" she asked. She'd read someplace that the longer you talked, the longer you lived.

"For the same reason I killed Gloria."

Tory felt some small satisfaction in knowing he had failed once, maybe he'd make the same mistake with her.

"But Gloria was involved with Evan, not with you."

She saw the total void in his eyes even as he smirked in apparent appreciation. "Gloria was *involved* with every one of us," Cal said with a snicker. "She wasn't a very choosy woman, if you get my meaning. Funny thing was, your father didn't see it."

"Maybe he saw something in Gloria the rest of you didn't." Tory longed to put the antagonistic words back in her mouth.

Apparently, Cal had the same thought, because she received a stinging blow from the back of his hand. Then she tasted blood and smelled her own fear.

"You're as dumb as your old man," Cal bellowed. "Even after Grif admitted he'd gone a round or two with Gloria, Bob was still smitten with her."

"Is that why you killed him? Because he was sleeping with Gloria?"

Cal let out a howl of laughter. "If I killed everyone that slept with Gloria, I'd still be reloading my pistol. Naw, Gloria was just an assistant. She got me to Evan, which was all I really needed."

"I still don't understand," Tory said just as she stumbled when her heel stuck in the metal grating. In the process of regaining her balance, she saw him. J.D. was a few yards behind them, slinking along the wall in his socks.

"Evan handled the money and the ordering. With his help and your father's own blind stupidity, I achieved my goal."

"Which was?"

"This isn't Twenty Questions, you stupid broad."

"I'd just like to know why my father died before you kill me."

Cal nodded and quickened his pace on the catwalk. "I connected Evan to some liquor suppliers. Bob was all for it, since the price was a whole lot lower than what he was getting from the wholesaler. And Gloria, she played her role by demanding little tokens of affection from your father. It was like taking candy from a sleeping baby."

"So my father spent the money he saved to buy Gloria gifts. That still doesn't explain why you killed him."

"That was his choice," Cal supplied. "I waited until I knew he was out of handy cash before I told him he was actually selling stolen liquor. Twenty-five grand would have kept my mouth closed. See—" Cal gripped her cheeks with viselike fingers "—back in those days, selling untaxed liquor carried a hefty fine, jail time and immediate revocation of your license to sell. I spend a year setting him up, he promises to pay. We agree to meet at the dependency—your father even had the cash. Then he had an attack of conscience. He starts threatening me," Cal scoffed. "Said he'd turn himself in and explain the circumstances. So, as you can see, I had no choice."

"Neither do I," J.D. said at the same time he lunged at the man, sending all three of them into a pile of entwined arms and legs. Tory ended up facedown, with her arms pinned beneath her.

Tory heard the distinctive sound of fist pounding flesh at least a half-dozen times before her body was crushed under a tremendous weight.

"J.D.?" she called out in a panic. "J.D!"

"It's over, doll," he said, rolling the unconscious Cal off her and gathering her to him.

The look in his eyes when he scanned her injured lip was indescribable. For an instant, Tory feared he might do more than just punch Cal.

Clutching his sleeve, her eyes met and held his. "It's over."

THREE HOURS LATER, she was soaking in a deep tub in one of the most posh rooms the Mirage had to offer. With her swollen lip and J.D.'s bloodied knuckles, they had agreed to stay in Las Vegas for a few days—long enough so that people would stop looking at them as if they were some strange couple into rough foreplay.

J.D. knocked before entering the bathroom. "Want some ice for your lip?"

"It's fine," she said, testing it with the tip of one finger. "How about your hand?"

The knuckles were red and raw, but he flexed his fist and said, "I've hurt them worse making a point to Wesley."

Tory laughed. "No wonder he became a psychiatrist. He's probably got some deep-seated phobia of being beaten to a pulp by older men."

"Wesley's phobia has nothing to do with men," J.D. confided. "Trust me. His troubles are solely of the female variety."

"Wesley's gay?" she gasped.

J.D.'s laughter reached all the way to his eyes. "Hardly. He's just overly picky when it comes to serious dating."

Tory felt the humor drain from her body. "Whereas you'll settle for whoever's handy?"

J.D. came to the edge of the tub and knelt beside her. "This is very hard for me," he began.

"Without the bubbles, I'm not doing very well myself."

His eyes flickered, giving her body a definitely approving perusal. "I could say I promise not to look, but that would be a lie. And I swear to you, Tory..." His voice caught and she patiently waited for him to finish. "I'll never lie to you again. Ever."

"Thank you." She gently stroked the side of his face, her heart filled with more love than she thought imaginable.

"There is something I'd like for us to do again, though."

"I want you, too," she said without hesitation.

"That's good to know, and we'll get to that."

"No, we won't, because I will have slit my wrists from the humiliation of having blurted out something like that."

J.D. reached behind him and produced a red velvet gift box. "I want you to marry me, Tory," he said as he opened the hinge on the box to reveal a stunning diamond engagement ring.

"We...we're already married," she stammered.

"But this time I'm asking you because I'm in love with you."

Tory smiled and it hurt. "I think we've done this whole thing backward."

"Is that a yes or a no?" he asked impatiently.

"Oh," she said, reaching for him. "It's a definite *yes.*"

WHEN THEY finally returned to Charleston three days later, J.D. knew no one would need a formal announcement that Mr. and Mrs. Porter shared more than just a name. And no one appeared happier than his mother, who greeted them at the airport along with Wes.

"I'm assuming from that simpleton grin on your face that you and Tory worked out your differences," Wes said.

"Completely," J.D. answered, hugging his wife to his side. "We even renewed our vows in one of those little chapels along the strip in Vegas." J.D. turned to his mother and said, "We used the Little Church of the West in your honor."

"The place Elvis married Ann-Margret in *Viva Las Vegas!*" Rose exclaimed.

"Don't worry, we have pictures. And a very fancy certificate." J.D. bent close to his brother's ear and added, "Which cost extra, if you can believe that."

Rose was definitely happy, but J.D. sensed something was bothering his mother. Later, when he invited her and Wesley up to the condo for a glass of wine, she still seemed distracted.

"What gives?" he finally asked, trying to ignore the way Tory was rubbing his thigh.

Rose clasped her hands together and said, "I'm afraid that if I tell you, neither one of you will ever speak to me again."

"No more lies," J.D. said firmly. "Or secrets."

Rose got up, went to her purse and dug out a dog-eared envelope, which she presented to him.

J.D. recognized the return address, pulled the letter from the envelope and burst out laughing.

"Aren't you furious?" Rose queried, resting her fists against her waist. "Read the date, J.D. I got that before the wedding."

"Got what?" Tory asked, taking the letter from him. She too began to chuckle.

"Don't either of you understand what that means?"

"It means," J.D. began as he brushed a kiss against Tory's temple, "that Tory's grandmother took care of all the paperwork years ago, and Tory had no claim to the Rose Tattoo, after all."

"Which means," Rose said, "you didn't have to marry her."

"Now that's where you're wrong, Mother," J.D. said with conviction. "I definitely had to marry Tory."

"Technically," Wes spoke up, "you've married her twice."

"Which I'm sure you'll find some sort of Freudian explanation for," J.D. retorted.

"It's here," Tory said, interrupting the never-ending sibling rivalry.

"What?"

"I got the grant," she told J.D. through a kiss.

"And you'll give it back," he said with a smile. At his wife's confused expression, J.D. explained, "Let them give the money to someone who really needs it. We can afford your last semester. I'm about to close a deal on an office complex in Tampa that will make your tuition look like pocket change."

"Wait!" Rose cried. "Does this mean you're going back to Florida when Tory finishes school?"

"No," J.D. answered. "We'll wait until after Christmas. Or maybe we'll stick around for Evan's trial. It's Tory's call."

Rose looked heartbroken. "But after all these years..."

"We'll visit one another and run up huge long-distance bills," J.D. promised. "My business in Florida is important to me, and Tory has agreed to relocate. But don't worry, Mom," he said as he stood and gave her a hug. "Wes has no real ties in Florida. There isn't a reason in the world why he can't move here."

"But if you have children," Rose grumbled.

"You'll be the first to know," J.D. promised.

Rose seemed somewhat placated by that. "I finally finagle myself a daughter-in-law, and she comes with a term limit."

J.D. kissed his wife before turning back to his mother and saying, "Then I suggest you cook something up for Wesley."

♥ SILHOUETTE
Intrigue

COMING NEXT MONTH

DARK STAR Sheryl Lynn

Mirror Images

Twenty-five years ago, Star Jones's parents had vanished. With no real evidence and no family to help her, she had to turn to private eye Austin Tack. Austin took her to more than an old, forgotten murder scene; they went on an emotional journey to discover her past. Because until Star found her past, how could she and Austin have a future?

UNDYING LAUGHTER Kelsey Roberts

Shadows and Spice

Destiny Talbott had more admirers than she could handle. Wesley Porter was intent on wooing her, but a second suitor was also vying for her attention…and his intentions seemed much more sinister. Wesley was determined to protect his lover from this dark stalker. He wanted the last date with Destiny!

FATAL CHARM Aimée Thurlo

Dangerous Men

He was tall, dark and dangerous… Not exactly the kind of man Amanda Vila was looking for as a father for her child. He was a renegade, thrown out of law enforcement because he was prepared to use any method to locate his kidnapped daughter.

But no other man had ever made her melt with desire—not like Tony amos.

WHAT CHILD IS THIS? Rebecca York

43 Light Street

Armed with nothing more than some vague memories and a grainy old photo, Travis Stone sought his parents. But first he found Erin Morgan. Once they had shared a love—a that love was now forbidden. For everywhere Travis searched he found dead ends—and dead men…

Travis had placed Erin in danger. He couldn't rest until he'd made her safe again.

COMING NEXT MONTH FROM
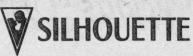 SILHOUETTE

Sensation
A thrilling mix of passion, adventure and drama

THE MORNING SIDE OF DAWN Justine Davis
LOVING EVANGELINE Linda Howard
IAIN ROSS'S WOMAN Emilie Richards
ANGEL AND THE BAD MAN Dallas Schulze

Special Edition
Satisfying romances packed with emotion

JUST MARRIED Debbie Macomber
BABY ON THE DOORSTEP Cathy Gillen Thacker
MORGAN'S MARRIAGE Lindsay McKenna
CODY'S FIANCÉE Gina Ferris Wilkins
NO KIDS OR DOGS ALLOWED Jane Gentry
THE BODYGUARD & MS JONES Susan Mallery

Desire
Provocative, sensual love stories for the woman of today

WOLFE WEDDING Joan Hohl
MY HOUSE OR YOURS? Lass Small
LUCAS: THE LONER Cindy Gerard
PEACHY'S PROPOSAL Carole Buck
COWBOY'S BRIDE Barbara McMahon
JUSTIN Diana Palmer

Delicious Dishes

Would you like to win a year's supply of sophisticated and deeply emotional romances? Well, you can and they're FREE! Simply match the dish to it's country of origin and send your answers to us by 30th November 1996. The first 5 correct entries picked after the closing date will win a year's supply of Silhouette Special Editions (six books every month—worth over £160). What could be easier?

A	LASAGNE			GERMANY
B	KORMA			GREECE
C	SUSHI			FRANCE
D	BACLAVA			ENGLAND
E	PAELLA			MEXICO
F	HAGGIS			INDIA
G	SHEPHERD'S PIE			SPAIN
H	COQ AU VIN			SCOTLAND
I	SAUERKRAUT			JAPAN
J	TACOS			ITALY

Please turn over for details of how to enter ☞

How to enter

Listed in the left hand column overleaf are the names of ten delicious dishes and in the right hand column the country of origin of each dish. All you have to do is match each dish to the correct country and place the corresponding letter in the box provided.

When you have matched all the dishes to the countries, don't forget to fill in your name and address in the space provided and pop this page into an envelope (you don't need a stamp) and post it today! Hurry—competition ends 30th November 1996.

Silhouette Delicious Dishes
FREEPOST
Croydon
Surrey
CR9 3WZ

Are you a Reader Service Subscriber?   Yes ❑   No ❑

Ms/Mrs/Miss/Mr _____

Address _____

_____

_____ Postcode _____

One application per household.

You may be mailed with other offers from other reputable companies as a result of this application. If you would prefer not to receive such offers, please tick box. ❑

C196
E